PRIEST

PRIEST

Ken Bruen

St. Martin's Minotaur
New York

www.minotaurbooks.com

Library of Congress Cataloging-in-Publication Data

Bruen, Ken.
    Priest / Ken Bruen.—1st U.S. ed.
        p. cm.
    ISBN-13: 978-0-312-34140-4
    ISBN-10: 0-312-34140-7
    1. Taylor, Jack (Fictitious character)—Fiction. 2. Private investigators—Ireland—Galway—Fiction. 3. Priests—Crimes against—Fiction.
4. Exorcism—Fiction. 5. Stalkers—Fiction. 6. Galway (Ireland)—Fiction.
I. Title.

PR6052.R785P75 2007
823'.914—dc22

                                                                2006039699

First published in Great Britain by Bantam Press,
a division of Transworld Publishers

First U.S. Edition: March 2007

10 9 8 7 6 5 4 3 2 1

For
Duane and Meredith Swierczynski, the
soul of Philadelphia,
and Tom and Des Kenny, the heart of the tribes.

An Sagart

. . . Priest

Those Blessed Hands
Anointed with the oil
Of final healing
The mystery of faith
Through decades now
Of pious full belief
Believed in you
Your fingers touching flesh
Of innocents
Who put their trust
In words no longer meaning anything but rape
And sodomizing
Sermonizing
Far beyond the Mount
Of any kind of ritual
You preyed upon
The bodies of the yet
Unformed
To desecrate
The temples of the barely grown
A predator in piety
Defiler from
The cross
To the very flock
You tended
Unholy is the writ
You've
Handed us in
Dust
The first initial of your name
Invokes the title of vocation
Torn in sacred text
Red blast across your mouth
To vomit
P . . . paedo—

PRIEST

1

*'What's wasted
isn't always
the worst
that's left behind.'*

KB

What I remember most about the mental hospital
     The madhouse
     The loony bin
     The home for the bewildered
is a black man may have saved my life.

In Ireland? . . . A black saves your life, I mean how likely is that? Sign of the New Ireland and perhaps, just perhaps, indication of the death of the old Jack Taylor. As I'd been for five months, slumped in a chair, a rug over my knees, staring at the wall. Awaiting my medication, dead but for the formalities.

     Gone but to wash me.

The black man leaned over me, tapped my head gently, asked,

     'Yo bro, anybody in there?'

I didn't answer, as I hadn't answered for the last months. He put his hand on my shoulder, whispered,

     'Nelson be in Galway this day, mon.'

     Mon!

My mouth was dry, always, from the heavy dosage.

I croaked,

'Nelson who?'

He gave me a look, as if I was worse than he'd thought, answered,

'Mandela, mon.'

I struggled to lift my mind from the pit of snakes I knew were waiting, tried,

'Why should . . . I . . . give a shit?'

He lifted his T-shirt – it had the Cameroon team on it – and I recoiled, the first stab of reality, a reality I was fleeing. His chest was raw, ugly, with the angry welts of skin grafts. White, yes, white lacerations laced his torso. I gasped, making human contact in spite of myself. He smiled, said,

'They was going to deport me, mon, so I set my own self on fire.'

He reached in his jeans, got out a ten-pack of Blue Silk Cut and a lighter, put a cig between my lips, fired me up, said,

'Now you be smoking too, bro.'

Bro.

That reached in and touched me deeply. Began the process of coming back. He touched my shoulder, went,

'You stay with me, mon, hear?'

I heard.

The tea trolley came and he got two cups, said,

'I put in de heavy sugar, get you cranking, fire your mojo.'

I wrapped my hands round the cup, felt the dull warmth, risked a sip. It was good, sweet but comforting. He was eyeing me closely, asked,

'You coming, bro? You coming on out of there?'

The nicotine was racing in my blood. I asked,

'Why? Why should I?'

A huge smile, his teeth impossibly white against the black skin. He said,

'Mon, you be sitting there, dat a slow burn.'

So it started.

I even went to the hospital library. It was tended by a man in his late sixties, wearing black pants and black sweatshirt. At first I thought the shirt had a white collar but to my horror saw it was dandruff. He had a clerical air, an expression of gravitas, as if he'd read the manual on librarians and went for the image. It was the one area in the whole place that was quiet, you couldn't hear the quiet anguish so evident in the other rooms.

I thought he was a priest and he stared at me, said,

'You think I'm a priest.'

He had a Dublin accent, which always has that tone of aggression, as if they can't be bothered with culchies (country yokels) and are prepared to battle with any peasant who challenges them. A question to a Dublin person is always interpreted as a challenge. I still wasn't used to speaking. You are silent for months, listening only to white noise, you have to struggle to actually make words. I wasn't intimidated, though, after what I'd endured, I wasn't about to allow some gobshite to bully me. Snapped,

'Hey, I didn't give you a whole lot of thought, fella.'

Let some Galway edge in there. What I wanted to say was, *Jeez, get some anti-dandruff shampoo*, but let it slide. He gave a cackle, like some muted banshee, said,

4

'I'm a paranoid schizophrenic, but don't worry, I'm taking my meds so you should be reasonably safe.'

The *reasonably* was a word to watch. He looked at his wrist, which was bare, and said,

'Is it that time already? Got to go get my caffeine fix. Don't steal anything – I'll know, I've counted the books twice.'

Stealing a book was truly the last thing on my mind, but if a Dubliner threatens you? The books were a mix of Agatha Christie, Condensed Reader's Digests, Sidney Sheldon and three Jackie Collins. A very old volume stood on its lonesome, like a boy who hasn't been selected for the team. I picked it up. Pascal, *Pensées*.

Stole that.

Didn't think I'd ever open it.

I was wrong.

I refused further medication, began to move around, my old limp hurting from the months of inactivity. I felt my eyes retreat from the nine-yard stare, move away from the dead place. After a few days, I was summoned to the psychiatrist's office, a woman in her late fifties named Joan Murray. She was heavily built but able to carry it, her hands were raw boned. A Claddagh ring on her wedding finger, heart turned in. She said,

'You've astounded me, Jack.'

I managed a tight smile, the one you attain when you first don the uniform of the Guards. It has no relation to humour or warmth but is connected to hostility. She leaned back, flexed her fingers, continued,

'We don't see many miracles here. Don't quote me, but

this is where miracles die. In all my years, I've never witnessed a restoration like yours. What happened?'

I didn't want to share the truth, afraid if I articulated it, it might revert. Said,

'They told me David Beckham was sold.'

She laughed out loud, said,

'That would do it. I've contacted Ban Garda Ni Iomaire – she brought you here, has stayed in touch about your condition.'

Ni Iomaire. Or Ridge, to use the English form. Daughter of an old friend, we'd been unwilling allies on a number of cases. Our relationship was barbed, angry, confrontational but inexplicably lasting. Like marriage. We fought like trapped rats, always biting and snarling at each other. How to explain the dynamics or disfunction of our alliance? Perhaps her uncle, Brendan Smith, had something to do with it. He'd been my sometimes friend, definite source of information and one-time Guard. His suicide had rocked us both. Against her inclinations, she'd become the source now. I'd helped her look good to her superiors, and maybe my being in her life kept his spirit alive. She was a loner too, isolated by her sexual orientation and on the edge. Lacking others, we clung to each other, not the partnership either of us wanted. Or what the hell, could be we were both so odd, so different that no one else would suffer us.

The doctor asked,

'Do you remember how you got here?'

I shook my head, asked,

'Can I have a cigarette?'

She stood, moved to a cabinet, got a heavy key chain

and opened it. You want to know the soundtrack of an asylum, it's the sound of keys. That and a low-toned moaning of the human spirit in meltdown, punctuated with the sighs of the lost. She took out a pack of B 'n' H, got the cellophane off, asked,

'These OK?'

I'd a choice? Said,

'They make you cough.'

And she laughed again. Took her a time to locate matches but she finally got me going, said,

'You're an alcoholic, Jack, and have been here before.'

I didn't answer.

What is there to say? She nodded as if that was affirmation enough, continued,

'But you didn't drink this time. Surprised? According to Garda Ni Iomaire, you'd been sober for some time. After the child's death . . .'

I bit down on the filter, froze her words.

After the child's death.

I could see the scene in all its awful clarity. I was supposed to be minding Serena May, the Down Syndrome child of my friends Jeff and Cathy. That child, the only real value in my life. We'd become close; the little girl loved me to read to her. It was a sweltering hot day, I'd opened the window of the second-floor room we were in. I'd been brutalized by a recent case and my focus was all over the place. The child went out the window. Just a tiny cry and she was gone. My mind just shut down after that.

I looked across the desk. She added,

'You were going into pubs, ordering shots of whiskey,

pints of Guinness, arranging them neatly and simply staring at the glasses.'

She paused, to let the fact that I hadn't actually drank sink in, then,

'Your Ban Garda brought you here.'

She waited, so I said,

'Fierce waste of drink.'

No laughter, not even a smile. She asked,

'What is the nature of your . . . friendship? With her.'

I nearly laughed, wanted to say *confron-fucking-tational*. But not an easy word to get your tongue round. When I said nothing, she said,

'You're leaving us tomorrow. Garda Ni Iomaire is coming to collect you. Do you feel you're ready to leave?'

Did I?

I stubbed out the cigarette in a brass ashtray. It had a hurler in the centre, the words

G.A.A. ANNUAL CONVENTION.

I said,

'I'm ready.'

She gauged me, then,

'I'm going to give you my phone number and a prescription for some mild tranquillizers, to help you through the first few days. Don't underestimate the difficulty of returning to the world.'

'I won't.'

She fiddled with her ring, said,

'You should attend AA.'

'Right.'

'And stay out of pubs.'

'Yes, Ma'am.'

A small smile. She stood, reached out her hand, said,

'Good luck, Jack.'

I took her hand, said,

'Thank you.'

I was at the door when she added,

'I'm a Liverpool supporter.'

I nearly smiled.

That evening, I had my first real meal with the general population. The atmosphere in the canteen was muted, almost religious. Long tables with near a hundred patients gathered. The joys of medication. I got a plate of sausages, mashed spuds and black pudding. I could taste the food, nearly enjoy it, till the TV was turned on. It stood above the room, attached to steel girders, locked down. What? Someone was going to steal it? The opening ceremony of Ireland's hosting of the Special Olympics. A wave of dizziness hit as the face of a special-needs child filled the screen. The reason I was here. Moving back from the table, I stood up. A woman with tangled black hair, nails bitten till blood had come, asked,

'Can I have your grub?'

Palpitations in my chest. A line of sweat coursed down my back, drenching my shirt. Serena May, the only light in an increasingly darkening life.

Dead.

Three years of age and gone because I lost my grip, wasn't paying attention. As I bolted from the refectory, a patient shouted,

'Yo, chow down.'

In my terror, I thought he said, 'Child down.'

Next morning I was packed, ready to leave. My holdall held trousers, one shirt and rosary beads.

The Irish survival kit.

Oh, and Pascal.

I went to find the black man, thank him for his help. I'd a pack of twenty cigs to give him. The doctor had included them with my tranquillizers. The black man was standing in the day room, staring at a newspaper. I mean staring as opposed to reading because the paper was upside-down. I'd learned his name was Solomon, went,

'Solomon.'

No reply.

I hunkered down, tried again. He had slid down along the wall. Slowly, his eyes reached up and he asked,

'I know you?'

'Yes, you pulled me back, remember?'

I offered the cigs and he gave me a petulant look, said,

'Don't smoke, boss.'

I wanted to touch his hand, but he suddenly emitted a piercing scream, then said,

'Fuck off, whitey.'

Later, months on, I rang the hospital to ask if maybe I might visit him, was told his deportation orders came through – the government was deporting eighty non-nationals a day. Using two wet sheets, freshly starched that morning, he hung himself in the laundry.

The new Ireland.

2

'Respect means, "Put yourself out."'

Pascal, *Pensées*, 317

1953. The rectory of a Catholic church in Galway.

The priest was removing his vestments, the altar boy assisting him. The priest lifted the glass of wine, said,
    'Try this, you've been a good boy.'
    The boy, seven years old, was afraid to refuse. It tasted sweet but put a warm glow in his stomach.
    His bum hurt and the priest had given him half a crown. Later, leaving the church, the priest whispered,
    'Remember now, it's our little secret.'

The nun was gathering up the song sheets. She loved this time of the morning, the sun streaming through the stained glass. Her habit felt heavy but she offered it for the souls in Purgatory. She found a ten-euro note in the end pew, was tempted to pocket it, buy a feast of ice cream. But blessing herself, she shoved it in the poor box. It slid in easily as the box was empty – who gave alms any more?

    She noticed the door to the confessional ajar. Tut-tutting,

she felt a tremor of annoyance. Father Joyce would have a fit if he saw that. He was a holy terror for order, ran the church like an army, God's army. Moving quickly, she gently pulled the door, but it wouldn't budge. Getting seriously irritated, she scuttled round to the other door and peered through the grille. Her scream could be heard all the way to Eyre Square.

Father Joyce's severed head was placed on the floor of the confessional.

The land of saints and scholars was long gone. In an era of fading prosperity, the mugging of priests, rape of nuns was no longer a national horror. It was on the increase. The deluge of scandal enveloping the Church had caused the people to lose faith in the one institution that had seemed invulnerable.

But the decapitation of Father Joyce brought a gasp from the most hardened cynics. The *Irish Times* editorial began with,

'We have been plunged into darkness.'

A leading Dublin drug lord offered a bounty for the capture of the killer. The Taoiseach gave a press conference asking for calm and understanding.

As if . . .

Ridge arrived in a yellow Datsun. Seeing my expression, she went,

'What?'

And we were back to our usual antagonistic relationship. The rare moments of warmth between us could be counted on the fingers of one hand, yet we continued to be joined together, our fates inexplicably bound despite our personal feelings. I smiled, wondering what had happened to basic civility, to a simple *How you doing?* gig. I said,

'The car . . . is it new?'

She was wearing tiny pearl earrings, a feature of Ban Gardai. Her face up close was plain but the vivacity of her eyes lent an allure. As usual, she was dressed a step above trailer trash, a small step. Penny's most loyal customer. White cotton jeans and a red T-shirt, the number 7 above the left breast. I wondered briefly if it was a sign, a sign to back one number in the lottery. Usually you got 5:1 on a single number. Dismissed it – superstition, the curse of my race.

You will never, and I mean *never*, catch an Irish person walking under a ladder or not crossing their fingers during a hurling match. Doesn't matter what you believe, it's as genetic, as casual as the use of the Lord's name. Sure it's bollocks but it's inevitable. She was instantly angry, shot back,

'Is that a dig?'

Meaning her sexual orientation. She was gay. I sighed, put my holdall on my shoulder, said,

'Fuck it, I'll hitch.'

'Don't you curse at me, Jack Taylor. Now get in the car.'

I did.

We drove in silence for almost ten minutes. She ground through the gear changes with ferocity, then,

'I've been wondering . . . After the . . . events . . . am, you went to the pub . . . ?'

She paused as she let a trailer enter a side road, continued,

'But you didn't actually drink?'

I checked my seatbelt, asked,

'So, what's your point?'

'Well, terrible things had happened, you'd ordered all those drinks . . . why didn't you actually lift a glass?'

I stared at the windscreen, took my time, then,

'I don't know.'

And I didn't.

If the answer satisfied her, the expression on her face wasn't reflecting it. Then,

'That means you're a success.'

'What?'

'You didn't drink. You're an alcoholic – not drinking makes you a success.'

I was flabbergasted, couldn't credit what she said.

'Bollocks.'

She glared through the windscreen, said,

'I told you, don't use that language. In AA they say if you don't pick up a drink, you're a winner.'

I let that simmer, hang over us a bit, noticed she had a St Bridget's Cross on the dash, asked,

'You're in AA?'

I'd never seen her really drink. Usually she had an orange, and one memorable time, a wine spritzer, whatever the hell that is. Course, I'd known nuns who turned out to be alcoholics and they were in enclosed orders!! Proving that, whatever else, alcoholics have some tenacity.

Her mouth turned down, a very bad sign, and she scoffed,
'I don't believe you, Jack Taylor, you are the densest man
I ever met. No, I'm not in AA . . . do you know anything?'
I lit a cig, despite the huge decal on the dash proclaiming,

DONT SMOKE

Not,

Please refrain from smoking.

An out-and-out command.
In response, she opened the windows, letting a force nine
blow in, turned on the air and froze us instantly. I smoked
on, whined,
'I've been in hospital. Cut me some bloody slack,' then
chucked the cig out the window.
She didn't close them, said,
'My mother is in AA . . . and you already know my uncle
had the disease . . . It has decimated generations of us. Still
does.'
I was surprised, understood her a little more. Children
of alcoholics grow up fast – fast and angry.
Not that they have a whole lot of choice.
We were coming into Oranmore and she asked,
'Want some coffee?'
'Yeah, that'd be good.'
If I thought she was softening, I was soon corrected as
she said,
'You buy your own.'

Irish women, nine ways to Sunday, they'll bust your balls. She headed for the big pub on the corner, which I thought was a bit rich in light of our conversation. The lounge was spacious and posters on the walls advertised coming attractions:

Micky Joe Harte
The Wolfe Tones
Abba tribute band.

I shuddered.

We took a table at the window, sunlight full on in our faces. A black ashtray proclaimed,

Craven A.

How old is that?

A heavy man in his sixties approached, breezed,

'Good morning to ye.'

Ridge gave him a tight smile and I nodded. She said,

'Do you have herbal tea?'

I wanted to hide. The man gave her a full look . . . like . . . was she serious, playing with a full deck?

'We have Liptons.'

'Decaffeinated?'

The poor bastard glanced at me. I had no help to offer. He sighed, said,

'I could give it a good squeeze – the tea bag, that is.'

Ridge didn't smile, went,

'I'd like it in a glass, slice of lemon.'

I said,

'I'll have a coffee, caffeinated, in a cup . . . please.'

He gave a large grin, ambled off. Ridge was suspicious, asked,

'What was that about?'

I decided to simply annoy her, said,

'It's a guy thing.'

She raised her eyes, went,

'Isn't everything?'

As is usual for Irish pubs, sentries sat at the counter – men in their sixties with worn caps, worn eyes, nursing half-empty pints. They rarely talked to each other and began their vigil right after opening time. I'd never asked what they were waiting for, lest they told me. If the sentries ever depart, like the monkeys on Gibraltar, the pubs will fold. The radio was on and we heard of a massive Garda drug sting in Dublin. For months they'd been scoring from dealers, now it was round-up time. There had been a public outcry when a TV camera filmed dealers selling openly on the streets and it was like a kasbah in Temple Bar. A junkie shooting up in front of a uniformed Guard. Crack cocaine was being sold widely. I said,

'Jeez, when crack arrives, the country is gone.'

Some irony for a nation that had given the word *crack* to the world – we now had crack of a whole more sinister hue.

She seemed not to have heard, then,

'Galway is as bad.'

'As if I didn't know.'

She was fiddling with a silver ring on her right hand, appeared nervous, asked,

'Did you hear about the priest?'

The question hung there, like an omen.

Like a sign of the times.

Ireland is a land of questions and very, very few answers. We're notorious for replying to a direct question with a question. It's like an inbred caution: never commit yourself. And it buys you time, lets you consider the implications of the query.

We may have got rich, but we never got impulsive. Questions are always suspect. The years of British rule, the years of *yes*, questions usually posed by a soldier with a weapon in your face, led to a certain wariness. If the truth be told, and sometimes it is, we really want to hit back with two other questions.

First, *Why d'you want to know?*

Second, and maybe more essential, *How is it any of your business?*

When I see a map of the island and they're promoting the country, like, say, for the tourist trade, they'll have a giant leprechaun or a harp, slap bang in the middle. I feel they should get honest and put a big question mark, let the folk know what they're letting themselves in for.

The classic Irish questions, of course, are the one to the returned emigrant, *When are you going back?* And the near daily one, *Do you know who's dead?*

Naturally, I didn't reply immediately to Ridge's question. Especially in the current climate. You hear about priests now, it ain't going to be good, it's not going to be a heartwarming tale about some poor dedicated soul who spent fifty years among some remote tribe and then they ate him. No, it's going to be bad, and scandalous. Every day, new revelations about clerical abuse. I can't say we'd become immune to that. The clergy will always hold a special place in our psyche, it's pure history, but their unassailable position of trust, respect and yes, fear, was over. Man, they'd had their day, and as the Americans might put it, *That is so, like, over.*

Was it ever.

3

'Of true justice. We no longer have any. If we had, we should accept it as a rule of justice that one should follow the customs of one's country.'

Pascal, *Pensées*, 297

We were on that stretch of road that leads into Galway. You could see the ocean on the left and, as always, it made me yearn – for what, I've never known. The silence in the car was oppressive and Ridge, in a very aggressive movement, flicked on the radio.

Jimmy Norman, Ollie Jennings were doing their two-hander on

    Sport
    Politics
    Music
    Craic.

I was homeward bound.

Jimmy said,

'Here's my favourite record.'

And Shania Twain launched with 'Forever And For Always'. I liked the line about never letting you go down. There wasn't a single human being I could think of who felt that way about me.

Years ago, watching Bruce Springsteen on video, Patti Scialfa had her eyes locked on him, a mix of adoration and ownership, centred on love. I knew, in a horrible moment of clarity, no one had ever gazed upon me so. I'd muttered, *'The awful knowledge of the wrath of God.'* Back in the pub, I had to shake myself physically, rid my mind of the demons. Must have shown in my face as Ridge's eyes softened, a rare occurrence. She asked,

'Jack, you OK?'

Jack!

A rib broke in the devil. I didn't answer and for one mad moment it seemed like she might reach out and touch me. Then she said,

'Jack, there've been some changes in Galway.'

I snapped out of the maudlin mode, said,

'Yeah?'

Like I gave a fuck.

She took a breath, then,

'Your friends, Jack and Cathy – she's gone back to London and he . . . Well . . . he's drinking.'

The parents of the dead child – my friends. Jeff had the alcohol deal, as I did. I could have asked about them, the fine hard details, but he was drinking, there was only one reply. So I let it slide, asked,

'How's Mrs Bailey?'

The owner of the hotel I'd been living in. Over eighty, she was a woman of true stature.

Ridge paused, then,

'The hotel was sold . . . And she . . . died a month ago.'

Sucker punch.

Like a blade in my gut. Once I muttered, a long time

ago, as I emerged from the DTs, *Everybody's dead, of fucking note perhaps.*

Ridge moved on, said,

'A friend of mine, she rented an apartment in the Granary, know it?'

Sure. I was a Galwegian, course I knew. The old Bridge Mills, like everything else, had been converted. Into luxury apartments. Looked out over the Claddagh Basin, view of the bay. What I mainly knew was they cost an arm and a leg. I asked,

'And this of interest, how?'

Couldn't keep the bitterness out of my tone: Mrs Bailey had been a bulwark in my life. Ridge was almost animated.

'She only stayed a week as her mother got sick and she had to go to Dublin.'

I lit another cig, blew the smoke through my nostrils, said,

'Fascinating as that is, it would probably be more gripping if I knew her. Thing is, is there a point to this?'

The anger crossed her face. She didn't fight it, replied,

'You're as insufferable as ever.'

I don't know who said it but it sure seemed now to fit.

'If a person is put in his place often enough, he becomes the place.'

I stretched and she went,

'Wait . . . okay?'

I did.

She continued,

'I'm trying to do you a favour here.'

I couldn't resist, snapped,

'And like, I asked you for a favour?'

The guy behind the bar was eyeing us warily. The vibe of hostility had obviously reached him. Ridge stood and we left. Outside, she handed me a key ring, two brass keys and a silver relic of St Therese. I smiled, couldn't help it. Other nations reach for weapons, we reach for relics. She smiled too.

'I got it at the Novena.'

I juggled the keys, said,

'To the Kingdom, I'd say.'

'Not exactly . . . for the Furbo Suite, my friend's apartment in the Granary. You have three weeks, get you sorted.'

'I've been months in a mental hospital. How much more sorted can I be?'

She'd no answer.

The fear hit the moment we reached Bohermore, the graveyard on my left. I kept my eyes averted. Tom Waits' 'Tom Traubert's Blues' began to unravel in my head . . . wasted and wounded.

Jesus.

I'd been married to a German, albeit briefly. She'd Rilke on the wall of her London apartment.

> 'Do not return. If you bear to, stay
> dead with the dead. The dead have their tasks.'

I'd thought ruefully many times, yeah, their task is to haunt me.

The poem is 'Requiem for a Friend'.

Ridge said,

'Galway has changed even in the short time you've been away.'

It looked like it usually did – unwelcoming. I said,

'Changed, not to be confused with improved.'

As if to mock my words, the sun appeared as we reached Eyre Square. It lit up the whole area – the crowds in the park, even the winos were animated. As we paused at the pedestrian crossing, streams of backpackers passed. Ridge was not impressed.

'We've just been voted the dirtiest city in Ireland.'

As a native, I wasn't surprised – the scarce litter bins seemed to function purely as urinals – but I didn't like the rest of the country to be in on the fact. Rough as my history in the town had been, it was the only town I had. Johnny Duhan's 'Just Another Town' captured the contradictions best. I answered,

'Dirtiest? And I don't suppose they meant the litter.'

She ignored that.

'A priest was beheaded.'

I couldn't resist, went,

'Not before time.'

Some years before, students had beheaded the statue of Padraig O'Conaire. Maybe it was contagious. We moved along past the newly refurbished Great Southern Hotel, turned right and up by the Skeffington Arms – it too had a facelift. Only the natives remained with the old faces. My flippant remark rattled her and she hit low, said,

'I knew him.'

What else could I do? I mumbled a lame apology but it cut no ice. She snapped,

'Sorry! Good God, you're always sorry, but are you repentant?'

Was I?

I considered a cig, but she was riled enough. Down past Moons, then a detour to drive the long route past the university, and again I averted my eyes. More bad history. Like Bono, I'd need permanent shades. Alas, they'd only dim the light, not the memory. We arrived in Dominic Street and she pointed to an alley beside Aran Travel, said,

'Go through there and the Granary is on the left. The Furbo Suite, your apartment, is on the top floor. No elevator, I'm afraid.'

I'd taken a heavy beating which involved my knee being hammered by a hurley. It left me with a limp, which wasn't as pronounced now but still noticeable. I turned to her.

'I'm very grateful, but I have to ask, why? Why are you helping me?'

She bit her lower lip.

'I might need a favour, and soon. And the apartment is vacant. It helps my friend and you need a place – it's not complicated.'

Of all the things I was sure of, that this would be complicated was one of them. So I asked,

'What's the favour you need?'

She was already putting the car in gear, snapped,

'Not now.'

I stood on the street as forlorn as I'd ever felt, the holdall at my feet, and watched her turn at the canal, disappear towards the west. She hadn't looked back.

Why would she?

The Furbo Suite amazed me. Contrary as I was, I'd resolved to be unimpressed. What was it, after all? Just another temporary shelter.

Got that wrong.

It was sensational. Decorated in pine, huge ceilings and truly luxurious. Beams criss-crossed the roof that had a comforting feel. There was a staircase. I'd of course anticipated one level. The bedrooms – yes, plural – were on the first level, then up the stairs to a wide open sitting room, surrounded by large windows. I gasped, went,

'Fuck.'

Best of all was the view. Out across the Claddagh, over the swans and the whole of Galway Bay in all its splendour. I loved it. Everything was provided: towels, iron, video, crockery, and a notice said the garbage was collected daily. I opened the fridge: milk, butter, a chicken, two steaks, chops.

Ridge, I figured.

I made some coffee and moved to a heavy oak armchair in front of the largest window, eased into it and stared at the view. I felt a hint of relaxation and slowly let out my breath. I hadn't even realized I'd been holding it. A phone on a small table nearby, and if I'd anybody to call, I'd have done so.

4

'We do not choose as captain of a ship the most highly born of those aboard.'

Pascal, *Pensées*, 320

CLERGY TOLD AVOID KIDS

Priests in a scandal-hit diocese have been warned to avoid contact with children while in public view. A code of conduct from the Ferns Diocese states clergy and volunteers should not be alone in a car, building or closed room with a young person.

The *Daily Mirror*, 26 June 2003

The priest case was heavy on my mind and I asked myself,
    'What do I care?'
    Priests and I hadn't exactly a good history, but you grow up Catholic, they have you. Deny all you like, they own your arse, and maybe my interest in this was because of my father. He always had respect for the clergy. He didn't like them – who did? But he used to say,
    'Their job isn't easy and *our* job is to support them.'
    I didn't believe that any more, but I still believed in him so I decided to have a look at the case. Just maybe, I could achieve one thing he might be proud of.

Was I deluding myself? You betcha. But it's what I do best, and who knew? I might even gouge back some iota of respect for my own self.

I scoured the libraries, collected all the back story I could. I read till my eyes hurt and I got what the Guards had gotten.

Nothing.

Did that deter me?

Did it fuck.

If it had been easy, I'd have left it there. I determined to stick with it. If I'd known then where this initial resolution would take me – into the heart of the Irish soul – would I have turned away?

Probably not.

I never did before.

That pain-in-the-arse adage about those who ignore the past being doomed to repeat it – they wrote that for me. If I'd known all the torments of the past, the lost love, the humiliation, shame and the oddest friendship on the face of God's earth that awaited me, would I have acted differently?

With knowledge aforethought, would I have said,

'Nope, not for me, thanks, I'll preserve what little sanity I have.'

Alas, I'd have still walked that road of unhappy destiny. Why?

Because I'm an eejit and, worse, a stubborn one.

Sister Mary Joseph was wringing her hands. It was her birthday, she was seventy years old, and though she never told anyone when the date fell, offering it up for the souls in Purgatory, she did allow for one treat each year – Häagen-Dazs, strawberry shortcake, large tub – and ate the whole shebang in one fell swoop. This year, she was too worried to eat. She was, in fact, worried sick. She'd known about Father Joyce's little temptations and had seen the altar boys crying, in obvious distress, but she had never told a soul. She was a nun, it wasn't her place.

As Father Joyce's *little temptations* grew uglier and more obscene, she had to bite her tongue and pray for guidance. She couldn't go up against a priest, it was unheard of, and so she stifled her conscience, turned a blind eye to the state of the altar boys. Now, with the murder of Father Joyce, she began to wonder if perhaps the madman might come after her. She took out her heavy rosary, stayed on her knees for hours, and still the fear and trepidation only increased. In bed that night, she cried for the boys, and for the loss of the ice cream too, melting away slowly beneath her bed. She could swear she heard it trickle.

I was standing at the Salmon Weir Bridge, seven in the evening. A late sun threw beams across the water. It made me yearn – for what I've never known, and probably never will.

Peace, perhaps.

You stand on that bridge and you get a sense of the sheer vibrancy of the city. When I grew up, it was a village – you knew everyone and, more important, they knew you. And as the saying goes in Ireland, they knew all belonging to you. If you had a brother in jail, they knew. If your sister was a nurse in England, they knew. It was truly parochial, with all the baggage that entails, the good and the bad. You couldn't have a pee without your neighbour being aware of it. But it also lent a spirit of care. When a family had trouble, the neighbours rallied round. There were no nursing homes to stash sick, elderly relatives in. This industry was a growth area now.

Nowadays, I could walk down the main street and not know one person. What you did notice was the sea of non-nationals. As a child, I never saw a black face outside of *National Geographic*.

More promising was the fact that a black woman, from Nigeria, was running for the city council. She hadn't a hope in hell, but give it time. I found that encouraging.

I saw a figure in black shuffling along like an injured crow, with smoke billowing behind. I wondered for a moment if I was hallucinating – they'd given me some pretty strong dope in the hospital and there were bound to be side effects, none of them good.

I wiped my eyes and realized it was a priest. Not just any priest but my nemesis, Father Malachy. I've hated few men as much as I hated him.

You're in some state, as a Catholic, when you hate a priest. They say there's a special place in Hell for priest-haters. The guy who took the head off the murdered priest, he was in for a real roasting. He'd be kebabbed.

My mother and I, we had a tortured relationship – she tortured me. And always in her miserable life there was Father Malachy, cooing and cajoling, leading her on to greater acts of piety. For piety, read interference in the lives of others. That I was drunk and a failed Guard was fuel for her daily martyrdom. He encouraged her in the belief and we had some epic battles. He usually got the last word in, and it was nearly always,

'God forgive you, because only God could.'

Nice, eh?

He looked like he usually did – as if he'd been pickled in nicotine. Last of the dedicated smokers, he lit one with another, and didn't even know he was smoking any more. It was as natural or unnatural as blinking. His face was deep lined, and his eyes were bloodshot. An air of desperation clung to him, or maybe I was just wishing that. He said,

'By the holy, 'tis the bold Taylor.'

And we were off.

I thought,

'Who needs this shite?'

Said,

'Fuck off.'

You use such words to a priest, you're already damned, but in my case, how much more damnation could they pile? The devil had me in hock to his arse as it was. I knew a little about philosophy, truth to tell I knew a little about most things. It was the bigger picture, as the Yanks say, that eluded me.

Sören Kierkegaard talked about man's condition on earth being *caught between insoluble tensions.*

Fucker nailed me.

Malachy stared at me and I snapped,

'What?'

'I need your help.'

I laughed out loud – not a laugh that had the remotest connection to humour or warmth, but the one you heard in the mental asylum, bred from pure despair. I asked,

'What, they caught you pilfering from the poor box?'

He leaned on the bridge, as if he needed physical support, said,

'I'm serious. That poor man who was beheaded . . . ?' and trailed off.

I shook my head, said,

'Don't tell me about it, pal, none of my business. You ask me, they're not beheading half enough of ye.'

He gathered himself, moved off, said,

'I'll talk to you again when you're sober.'

I roared,

'I'm not drinking.'

And wished I was.

He paused, then,

'Why do you never address me correctly?'

'What?'

'I'm a priest, you should address me as Father.'

'You're not my father. Christ on a bike, that you should be anyone's father. What a curse that would be.'

If he'd called me son, I'd have thrown him to the salmon. Little did I know my whole life was about to be immersed in the whole father-and-son dynamic of – should that read, *dysfunction*?

Remember Cat Stevens, a very successful singer-songwriter who returned to his Islamic roots and changed his name? They'd re-released his classic song, 'Father And Son'.

The fates, you might say, were fucking with me big time, but was I listening? Was I fuck.

On the bridge, to my left, was the cathedral. Some irony that it had previously been the city jail. Further along was the university, and you could hear the high jinks of the students, carried along a stray breeze. Staring down into the water, you could see the salmon, swimming against the tide, like meself. Our new prosperity had added the obligatory pollutants and the fish were as diseased as my nature. It never ceased to lift my spirits a bit to watch those beautiful salmon, almost swaying against the current. Made you almost wish to be a poet.

A fella passing quipped,

'Don't do it, tomorrow's another day.'

I thought I'd need that in writing.

Everyone's a comic, and in Galway, more comics than most anywhere. I sighed. I lit a cig from a box of safety matches, flicked the match over and watched it drift towards the water. I could see three fine salmon, their gills moving easily. Pollution was killing more and more of them.

Two men approached, weaving slightly. I recognized them from Jeff's pub. I'd usually nod, say hello, nothing too personal. The rules of pub behaviour – you could see a guy for twenty years thus and never trade more than a handful of sentences.

The rules were off.

Because they were drunk. The other side of a feed of Guinness, Jameson chasers, how I drank myself. The first, in a grubby Aran sweater, was your good-natured drunk –

a few pints, everyone was his mate. The second, a different animal. Wearing a Mayo football shirt, he was mean and primed. Booze only justified a rage that he wore always. Aran said,

'Taylor! I thought you'd left the country.'

The other glared. I said,

'Keeping a low profile.'

Mayo looked like he was going to spit, had hawked a mouthful of phlegm, was swirling it, said,

'Hiding out, more like.'

I knew what was coming, turned round to face him, asked,

'What's that mean?'

He spat close to my shoe, looked at Aran, decided it was safe, said,

'You killed a kid, hadn't the balls to face people.'

I hit him high on the chest, above the heart. Taught to me on the streets of Armagh by a Sinn Fein activist, it's a sucker punch. Bring the strength from your feet, brace your toes and use an easy flow to let it travel almost lazily with maximum impact. His mouth opened in a slight 'O' and he sank to his knees, a dull sheen to his eyes. I had to forcibly restrain my shoe from connecting with his head. Christ, I so wanted to finish the job.

Aran was stunned, muttered,

'Jesus, Jack.'

My first name now? Violence begets respect.

I flicked my cig high above the bridge, cool or what? I put a man down but never dropped the cig, surely that impresses someone? I turned and walked away. The violence began to leak, seep from my pores. At Eyre Square, I had to sit down, as the inevitable shakes and drained vibe hit. Across the square, I could see the Skeff, like a beacon. I could make it over, hammer in a large Paddy, chill on easy. I nearly smiled. I'd just hammered a small Paddy.

Next morning I woke, amazed to be sober. Oh, I'd wanted to drink, and so badly, to submerge in Jameson for ever. Got out of bed and tried to figure out what the hell the noise was, surrounding me. Then I realized – the water, like a train heard in the distance. I'd been reared in Galway, between canals, close to the ocean, but had never consciously heard it. The old mill and the proximity inten-sified the sound. It was comforting, like a prayer you know is about to be answered. I showered, shaved, put on a clean white shirt, newish jeans I couldn't recall buying, and brewed up a steam of coffee. Took the mug to the table, sat. If I'd gone to the window, I knew I was likely to spend hours staring at the bay. The view had a soporific, mesmer-izing effect, not too distant from healing, a visual therapy.

I thought of the incident the night before and resolved to curb my rage, if I could. Else I'd spend my time beating on people. How to re-enter life and act as if I wanted that? My previous years I'd spent as a half-assed private investi-gator, finding people, solutions, mostly fuelled on alcohol. Time after time, I'd been plunged into horror, disaster, and lost everyone I cared about. The list of my dead would cover a wall. Entertained that mad notion, get a red marker, list them all. The very idea gave me a shudder and I was up, pushing them away.

I turned the radio on, in time for the news. The top story was George Best. Only months since he received a new liver and he was drinking again. The operation had lasted thirteen hours and needed forty pints of blood. There'd been violent opposition to an alcoholic receiving the transplant. *There were so many more deserving cases.* An old debate, always volatile . . . *Why help an alkie when he'll only drink again?*

Various experts were giving their views/opinions on *why* he'd do such an insane thing. The whole report contained an air of bafflement as to his behaviour. I shouted,

'What's the matter with ye? He's an alcoholic, what's the bloody mystery?'

Realized I was dangerously angry. In the hospital, there'd been compulsory AA meetings. Catatonic as I was, they wheeled me along. I remembered the admonition – don't get too angry, too lonely, too tired.

Switched the radio off, took a few deep breaths then got a pen, some paper and outlined my finances. Figured I'd enough to last a few weeks if I didn't eat, so conclusion,

> Get a job.

Then added

> Get a life.

Could picture placing an ad in the paper, to go

> Drunkard
>
> Early fifties
>
> Recently released from mental asylum
>
> Seeks gainful employment.

Yeah, that'd work.

I got item 8234, my all-weather Garda coat, and headed

out. I had no plan, which in itself was a whole new country. A slight drizzle was starting and I turned up my collar, my knee wasn't aching so the limp was less apparent. Still, I took it slow and went over the canal, hit Quay Street from the wild end. Wild in the sense of it being where most revellers collapsed. Outside Jury's, I recognized a tinker who'd recently *settled*. Moved from a caravan to a house. He was wearing a shiny black leather jacket and his black hair was awash with gel. These jackets were everywhere, a family of Romanians having snuck them into the country. His face was deep brown, lined from the elements and cigs. He fell into step beside me, muttered the Irish benediction,

'Sorry for your trouble.'

A whole selection right there. Could be my mother's death, the mental hospital, the tragedy of Jeff and Cathy's child or my damn sorry existence. I played it vague, said,

'Thanks, Mick.'

He had his hands buried in his pockets, said,

'Isn't it a hoor?'

I needed a little more to work on, so asked,

'What's that?'

'We were beaten again, by one lousy point.'

Hurling.

I hadn't even known Galway were playing, how removed was I? The sports channel doesn't get a lot of viewers in the asylum – the big favourite are the soaps. Proves the patients need their meds upped. I did the Irish dance, asked,

'And you're keeping well?'

This neatly encapsulates

Family

Employment

Health.

He wheezed as if requested, took his right hand out of his pocket, reached to touch a Miraculous medal round his neck, said,

''Tis my chest, the fags have me killed.'

'Did you try the patches?'

He shrugged off this nonsense, said,

'They should bring out a patch for the drink.'

I thought Antabuse was much the same deal, but said,

'Not a bad idea.'

He stopped, creased his eyes, said,

'Man, if you had one, say of whiskey, you could just tap it – you'd have a drink without having to buy a bottle.'

I smiled and he said,

'A fella could make a fortune.'

When brewers were already targeting teens with alcohol-flavoured water and sundry varieties of 'attractive' liquor, I felt the country had enough methods of downing booze, but said nothing. In Ireland, no reply is taken for agreement. He asked,

'You'll have heard about Father Joyce?'

'Yes.'

'Cut the head off him, the poor bastard.'

I hadn't a whole lot to add, so did the required, said,

'May he rest in peace.'

Mick couldn't resist, said,

'Or . . . pieces.'

Then, as if to take the harm out if it, added,

'God forgive me.'

We'd reached Kenny's Bookshop, a display of Irish literature in the window. I hadn't read in months – maybe I'd be able to do so now. Mick said,

'The fella who strangled the old nun, remember, two years ago?'

Not an event easily forgotten. I nodded and he said,

'He got life. I saw him on TV yesterday – he didn't look a bit sorry.'

Ireland had changed irrevocably. In my youth, the clergy had been bulletproof. Now it seemed to be open season. I asked,

'Is that weather guy on TV3 . . . he still around?'

A forecaster who managed the impossible, made Irish weather seem decent.

Mick was delighted. I'd hit a home run, asked,

'Do you like him? Isn't he fucking gifted.'

The ultimate Irish accolade, bestowed rarely. The weather man had a cheesy American style of delivery, humanized the forecast. Sure, it was going to lash down but it wasn't malicious, not like England. But hey, what could the weather do? It had to rain, it was Ireland, our birthright, kept the grass green and ensured we'd always have a grievance.

I asked Mick if he was all right for a few bob and he assured me he was good, but then in a serious vein went,

''Tis none of my business, but your poor mother's grave, it's in a shocking state.'

I didn't want to go there, said,

'Oh.'

He was being as careful as he could, but some issues had to be addressed. He continued,

'I know you . . . haven't been . . . well . . . But you know, people talk.'

Like I gave a fuck. I said,

'I appreciate your concern.'

I didn't.

He wasn't quite finished, said,

'My cousin Tomas, he does graves, does a lovely job. I could have a word.'

I agreed, reached for my wallet. He blew it off, said,

'Settle up another time. You have always been a friend to our people.'

Which might be the best epitaph I can get.

5

'Cause and effect. One must have deeper motives and judge accordingly, but go talking like an ordinary person.'

Pascal, *Pensées*, 336

A week later, I went for a job interview, as a security guard. I knew how ridiculous this was – I was applying to mind buildings and I couldn't mind myself. As my mother had been fond of saying, after I became a Guard,

'Him! A Guard! He couldn't mind mice at a crossroad.'

I have to admit that particular image always made me smile, not what she intended. In Ireland, possibly the greatest sin is to have ideas above your station. Notions, they're called, to 'lose the run of yourself', as they say. She ensured I never did.

The security office was located at the rear of the Augustinian church, close to Galway's only sex shop. Tempting to say, keep your vices close. Yeah, we had our first sex emporium. They follow in the wake of the big boys: McDonald's, River Island, Gap. I'm not sure of the implications, other than money, but they are the bottom feeders.

The sun was splitting the rocks. Europe was being blasted by a heatwave, England baking in the high thirties, Tony Blair feeling heat of a different kind as he clung to his 'We'll find weapons of mass destruction' dogma. In Ireland, we had our own weapon of mass destruction.

Alcoholism.

I was wearing a short-sleeved white shirt, a dark-blue tie, loosely fastened – that careless-swagger touch, black pressed pants, sensible black slip-on shoes. All purchased from the Vincent de Paul shop, cost me all of nine euro. The woman behind the counter held up the shirt to the light, looked at me, assessing, said,

'That'll be lovely on you.'

Well, it fit.

The shoes were too tight but a daily level of discomfort

>Physical

>Mental

>And/or

>Spiritual

was habitual.

Time was, when I read Thomas Merton, found uplift there. Not no more. A corrosive despair rendered him obsolete. What the shoes did was emphasize my limp. Perhaps I'd get the sympathy vote, be employed on a variation of the disabled-vet syndrome. What I knew of security firms I'd mostly gleaned from my dead friend Brendan Cross. He'd once told me,

'If you can stand up, you can be a security guard.'

I'd asked,

'That's it?'

'Helps if you're under seventy.'

The guy who interviewed me was definitely sixty. He'd obviously watched a lot of bad B movies, as a cigar stub, unlit, was lodged in the corner of his mouth. He rotated it slowly as he spoke, said,

'I see from your application you were a Guard.'

I nodded, not volunteering further. That I'd been bounced wasn't a selling point.

He made various grunts, whether of approval or not I couldn't tell. To say my papers were sketchy was putting it mildly. He sighed, asked,

'When can you start?'

'Am . . .'

'You free today?'

I was free every day, but fuck, I hadn't got my head ready to jump so fast. I said,

'I'm moving house, could I start next week?'

He finally looked at me. I hoped the white shirt was strutting its stuff and I said,

'Give you time to check my references.'

My referees were Ridge and a doctor who'd once set my broken fingers. The guy said,

'Whatever.'

I realized the interview was over, stood, said,

'Thank you for your time.'

'Yeah, yeah.'

I left, thinking,

'I'm employed, just like that?'

Decided to go to the Augustinian, light a candle for all my dead. I used to bring my business to the Abbey but they'd priced themselves out of the market. Their rates for Mass Card signings had gone way up. At the church, I dipped my fingers in the Holy Water font, blessed myself, intoned . . . *In ainm an Athair* . . . the Lord's Prayer in Irish. Mass was just concluding and there was a sizeable crowd. I went to St Jude's shrine at the back and put some money in the box. I was sad to see the candles were now automated. You pressed a button and a light came on. What a shame. The whole deal of actually selecting a candle, lighting it, had been a ritual of comfort, as old as poverty. What next? Internet access, sit at home, light a candle on a website. I chose a position on the top right, hit the button, didn't work. Tried three more. Nope. Hoped it wasn't an omen, knelt and said,

'For the repose of the souls of the dearly departed.'

Felt like a hypocrite. An old woman came in, put her coins in the box, hit a button and the whole top row lit up. She seemed delighted. I wanted a refund. Maybe I hadn't put the right money in, was it *exact fare only* or was there a special offer, ten lights for only €9.99? It was too complicated. I got out of there, a sense of unfulfilment in my heart.

Stood on the steps, the sun on my face, heard,

'Mr Taylor? Mother of God, is it yourself?'

Janet, the chambermaid/pot walloper/all-round staff at Bailey's Hotel. She had always looked as old as Mrs Bailey, got to be hitting late eighties. Wearing a Connemara shawl, she looked frail. Those shawls were made by hand, handed down from mother to daughter, a slice of living history. I said,

'Janet.'

And she moved, gave me a full hug, said,

'We heard you were in the madhouse.'

Paused, blushed, tried,

'Oh heavens, I mean the hospital.'

I hugged her back, said,

'I was but I'm OK now.'

She released me, uttered the closest thing to an Irish benediction.

'Let me have a look at you.'

Centuries of care in that. And *look* they do, but with tenderness, concern. She said,

'You need fattening up.'

I smiled, asked,

'How are you?'

Her face lit up, much like the top row of candles. Excitement in her eyes, she exclaimed,

'Isn't it great?'

What?

I was lost, went,

'I'm lost.'

She moved in close, as if eavesdroppers were everywhere, which in Ireland they probably were, near whispered,

'About our legacy.'

My face was showing my confusion and she said,

'Mrs Bailey had no children, no close ties. So she left me money and before she died, may she rest in peace, she told me she was leaving you a small flat and money.'

I was stunned, lost for words. Janet rooted in a brand-new leather handbag – the result of the legacy, I suspected – found a business card, handed it over, said,

'That's the solicitor, he's anxious to hear from you.'

I read the name:

Terence Brown
Family solicitor

with four phone lines.

I said,

'I'll call him.'

Janet was smiling, but with a sadness in her eyes said,

'Mrs Bailey said you'd been a great help to her, and she worried about you having a home.'

I had to ask,

'Where is she buried?'

'Fort Hill, beside her husband.'

There are three cemeteries in Galway: Bohermore, Rahoon and Fort Hill. I had friends and family in the first two. Few people were buried in the third any more, you had to be very old Galway. Even in death, there are categories. Janet checked a new gold watch, said,

'I'll have to go, Mr Taylor, get my husband's dinner.'

I'd never met him but asked,

'How is he keeping?'

Her reply contained all the casual warmth and affection of a lost era, almost thrown away in its simplicity.

'Sure what would be wrong with him? We have Sky Sports, there's not a brack on him.'

Another hug and she was gone. I hadn't said we'd be seeing each other – our relationship didn't entail commitment. I shook myself, amazed at how my day was shaping. Not yet noon and I'd a job, perhaps a home and even the prospect of money. What it did was make me want to celebrate, and I'd only ever known one way to do that.

Drink.

I walked up to Eyre Square, took a seat near the fountain, let the sun wash over me, wondered to whom should I say thanks.

The Square was hopping.

Backpackers

Office workers

Children

Apprentice hooligans

Winos

The homeless.

Time was, Buckfast was the very bottom of the booze chain. Regarded as but a notch above meths, known as the Wino's choice . . . cheap and potent. Lately, teenagers had discovered if you mixed it with Red Bull and a shot of cider, you got wasted. This new popularity had caused a price hike. Under my bench, I counted four empty bottles. Had I ever drunk it?

Undoubtedly.

Near the pay-toilets, a drinking school was huddled. A bunch of men and women, ragged, dirty, subdued. At intervals, they'd send forth an emissary to perform the 'beg'. The rules of the school were simple: don't return empty handed. On a bench beside them, one of their number sat alone, his head down. A tremor discernible across the distance. He shook his head and something in the movement chilled my heart. I got up, began to approach. The school, seeing me, sent a scout who went,

'Spare change for a cup of tea, Sir?'

I waved him off and he veered to my left, targeted a German couple scanning a map.

I stood over the man, went,

'Jeff?'

No answer, then slowly his head came up, the once fine long hair now knotted, dirty. Sores lined his mouth, a fading bruise covered his left eye. An odour rose from his body, a mix of urine, damp and decay. He focused, croaked,

'Jack?'

I wanted to embrace him, get him a bath, fresh clothes. I asked,

'What can I do, buddy?'

I didn't hear his reply and leaned closer. His breath smelled like a dead horse. He muttered,

'Go fuck yourself, Jack Taylor.'

I reeled back and he tried to straighten, then spat near my foot, said,

'Killed my golden child.'

6

*'Between us and heaven or hell there is
only life halfway.'*

Pascal, *Pensées*, 213

The weirdest thing had happened. The night before, I'd dreamed of Ridge, and though it kills me to say it, in a, Jesus, romantic way. How fucked is that?

In the dream, she was in my arms and I was holding her as tight as a rosary. She turned her face for me to kiss her and then . . . Oh God, I woke up, feeling guilty, exhilarated, confused, angry – the usual morning baggage. Worse, I could still sense her touch in my arms and missed it. There's no fool like an old sodden one. I think my face reddened as I realized I'd been happy.

Of all the screwed-up notions to get, this was among the worst. I was what? Going to fall in love with the one woman who was totally unavailable to me on every level. I hated meself more in those few moments than usual, and I had a very full quota of self-loathing. I resolved to bite down on whatever crazy impulse this was and to extinguish it at every possible moment. If I was ever insane enough to share this mad dream with her, I could just picture her face, full of pity and disgust. That picture will wipe out love fairly fast.

It unnerved me and that's the holy all of it.

I got hold of the dictionary, looked up the word I needed and yeah, it fit.

Armed thus, I used it aloud, muttered,

''Twas nothing but an aberration.'

Did that help?

Yeah, right.

There is one cure for most ailments, a sure-fire method to jolt you back to reality, and it's so Irish, it's like a cliché, or worse, an Irish joke.

It's the graveyard.

Fort Hill is close to the docks. You look north and the Radisson Hotel looms close. Lough Atalia spreads out before the entrance to the graveyard. I'd bought a bunch of flowers – red and white roses – and, self-conscious, crammed them into a holdall. It was another fine day. At this rate, we might have the makings of a half-assed summer. Course, the rain is never far behind, but it lures you into a false sense of security. Buy new summer gear and presto, winter arrives in the middle of June. We do get all the seasons in Ireland, it's just they all arrive on the same day.

I moved among the graves till I found a small marker with

Mrs Bailey.

A headstone, if there was to be one, wouldn't go up for a year. Withered wreaths lay in the area. I added my crushed roses – if nothing else, they brought a flash of colour. I

never knew what to do at a graveside. Do you kneel or
stand, look solemn . . . what? I muttered,

'You were a real lady of real class.'

Does that qualify as a prayer? It was at least the truth.
I saw a figure in black approaching and said,

'Priest at nine o' clock.'

As he drew near, I saw him draw deep on a cig then flick
the butt into a cluster of headstones. I'd wanted a cig badly
but felt you didn't smoke in a churchyard. I recognized him
– Father Malachy, my mother's constant companion.

In Ireland, there's a curious . . . what am I saying? The
whole country is crammed with oddities. Among them is
the single woman/priest phenomenon. Females of a certain
age – over fifty, usually – adopt a priest, become his constant
companion and no one seems to question it. Try adopting
a nun. The assumption is made that it is above board. In
truth, it rarely seems to be sexual, but how the hell would
I know? What I do know is that it is accepted.

Some women get pets, others opt for tame clergy. Malachy
belonged to my mother, as if they were joined at the hip.
They certainly agreed on one thing, that I was a

> Loser
> Drunkard
> Ne'er-do-well
> Blackguard.

Friendships have flourished on less.

I hadn't seen him since the night on the bridge and, to
be honest, I don't think he'd once crossed my mind. A big
man, he was again enclosed in a haze of nicotine. I've never
seen such a dedicated smoker. Not that they appeared to

give him any pleasure. On the contrary, they acted like an accelerant on his already short fuse. Watching him suck a cig was horribly fascinating. He drew on it with ferocity, his cheekbones bulging, his eyes near sunk in his head. The anti-smoking lobby could put him on their posters, he'd be a powerful deterrent. He said,

'Taylor.'

I decided to use his full title, let a little edge in it, went,

'Father Malachy.'

Threw him. He was wearing the obligatory black, the dog collar visible above a heavy black sweater. Sweat was rolling off him. I said,

'I didn't know this was your patch.'

We were obviously going to act as if the incident on the bridge had never occurred. Fine by me, denial was my strong suit.

'I saw you coming in.'

'And what, you followed me? Being tracked by a priest, I'm not sure it's a good thing, not to mention a little unusual.'

Whatever was going on with him, it was making him very nervous. He said,

'I need your help.'

The exact same words as before.

The words near strangled him, he had to force them out between his teeth. I wasn't about to assist, said nothing. Left, as the psychologists say, the black hole, let him fill it. A plain-clothes Garda had once told me that silence is the best interrogation tool. People can't stand it, they have to fill that void.

He did.

Rooted for his cigs, fired one up, asked,

'Can I buy you a drink?'

And saw my face. He – who'd castigated me for years on the booze – tried to recover, faltered, altered,

'I mean, tea . . . or coffee. We can go to the Radisson, 'tis a fine hotel.'

They also had a no-smoking edict. The Services Industry was currently locked in a bitter fight with the Government. From 1 January 2004, smoking would be prohibited in pubs, restaurants, public buildings. The ban in the first two would, the industry claimed, kill tourism dead, not to mention local trade. Smokers couldn't imagine a visit to the pub without nicotine and vowed to stay home.

Malachy was still holding his cig as we sat in the pristine lounge. A waiter approached, glanced at the smoke, didn't lay down the law. Priests still carried some clout. We ordered a pot of coffee. Malachy added,

'Put some biscuits on a plate, take the bare look off it, that's a good lad.'

The lad was at least thirty-five.

I'd never really looked at Malachy, I'd never thought about his age or his appearance. It's an awesome thought to realize you've dismissed a person in his entirety because you loathe him. Now I'd guess his age at late fifties, and from the pallor in his face, the expression in his eyes, hard years, all of them. He had a full head of hair, streaked with grey, not recently washed. He had the hands of a navvy, like a character from a Patrick McGill book. Old Galwegians would have described him as a bacon-and-cabbage man, with a truck of spuds on the side, dripping with butter. He'd have followed that with a dish of stewed apple, gallon of thick custard. His type had built the roads of England.

The coffee came with a plate of Rich Tea biscuits. Malachy barked,

'Hope they're fresh.'

The waiter nodded, too dumbfounded to reply. Malachy grabbed the bill, examined it, went,

'Jaysus.'

I went to reach for my wallet but he blew that off, produced a crumpled note, handed it over. The waiter looked at him expectantly but no tip was forthcoming. I poured the coffee, the aroma was good and strong. I asked,

'Milk?'

Malachy was shovelling biscuits into his mouth, the cig still going. I wanted to ask,

'Missed breakfast?'

But we'd enough friction going. He asked,

'Did you hear about Father Joyce?'

The beheaded priest. I nodded and he said,

''Tis an awful business.'

Which was some understatement. He stared into space, then suddenly changed tack, asked,

'What was it like in . . . the, am . . . hospital?'

I knew the term *madhouse* had been on the tip of his tongue. I said,

'Quiet. It was surprisingly quiet.'

He risked a look at me, then another biscuit, said,

'I was always afraid of those places, I thought there'd be fierce screaming.'

I thought about that, said,

'Oh, there was screaming, but it was silent. The wonders of medication. And for me, they provided what I most wanted – numbness.'

And I realized that in the current jargon, I was *sharing*, with a man I despised. Not that I'd anyone else. The past few years had annihilated near all I'd known, friends and family. You need a whole new level of numbness to wipe that slate. To my own surprise, I asked,

'Being a priest, how's that?'

I don't know if it's pc, if you're allowed to ask such a question, but we'd entered territory new to us both. He finished the biscuits, wiped his mouth with his sleeve, said,

'It's a job. Not one I'd have picked.'

So you have to ask, get it out there.

'Doesn't it work the other way? You're the one who's supposed to be . . . as you put it, picked?'

Another cig going. I hadn't wanted one since meeting him, he was more effective than the patch. He gave a laugh full of malice and anger, not an easy blend. He said,

'My mother, Lord rest her, it was her fervent wish I be a priest. She thought it was a real blessing on the family.'

The expression *black with rage* had always seemed just that – an expression. I swear his face was slate in temper. I tried to change the subject, asked,

'How can I help you?'

He pulled himself back from whatever abyss he'd seen, touched the empty plate like a blind man, looking for crumbs or hope, I don't know. I recognized that huge hunger, the thirst that underlines the emptiness within. I'd used booze to fill mine – it hadn't worked. Maybe nicotine was his method. He said,

'The Archdiocese are very concerned about the ramifications of Father Joyce. There were rumours about . . . abuse.'

I sighed. The country was still reeling from five years of horror at the number of clergy who'd been accused, arrested and convicted of the most shocking child abuse. Case after case, the level of suffering inflicted was almost beyond comprehension. The most notorious, Father Brendan Smith, who was convicted and died in prison, had, on his conviction, turned to the TV cameras and showed a face devoid of any remorse. They buried him at night, which is its own verdict. Another priest, also convicted, on being bundled into the police car gave the cameras the two-finger gesture. It didn't take an expert to gauge the rage of the people.

I ran all that in my head, asked,

'What on earth do you think I can do?'

He was nervous now, fidgeting in his seat.

'You've had success before, cases that were closed. You found . . . solutions.'

I'd just gotten a job, maybe a real place to live, an actual inheritance. I didn't need this. I asked,

'What about the Guards?'

He shook his head.

'We need this to be discreet. The last thing we want is a high-profile investigation.'

'But surely there's already that.'

He turned to me, pleading.

'Jack, Father Joyce was . . . accused . . . of molestation . . . some years ago. We have to keep this in house.'

What a term. The Church had protected abusers before, abused the accusers and transferred the culprit to another parish. Reassigned a suspected monster to a new and unsuspecting populace. I asked,

'Have you the names of the accusers?'

He reached in his pocket, took out a sheet of paper, laid it on the table, said,

'I knew you'd help, Jack.'

I snapped,

'Didn't say I would.'

I thought I detected a rare smile, but it was gone before I could react. I took the paper, three names and addresses, asked,

'Supposing, just supposing, I find the man, can even prove it. Then what?'

Malachy was standing.

'We'll hand him over to the authorities.'

Nothing in his eyes led me to believe there was a scrap of truth in that.

We went outside and the sun was still high in the sky. I turned to him, said,

'You're a bad liar.'

'What?'

His face already confirming my intuition, I said,

'This is nothing to do with the Archdiocese, that doesn't make sense. It's to do with you.'

He stared at his shoes, then,

'I'm afraid.'

'Why?'

It seemed he was close to hyperventilating.

'I was accused . . . Two years ago . . . The same awful thing.'

Sweat popped out on his forehead, began to pool, then slowly ran in thin streams down his face, like the beads on a rosary and twice as significant. He was shaking.

'Being a priest is like being crucified without a cross, you know that – raked with such longings . . .'

The word *longings* carried such heavy sexual connotations that I moved back a step, my mind grappling with him doing . . . stuff to boys.

He rushed on, desperate to get it out.

'And sure, sometimes you'll see a boy . . . the innocence, they look like angels . . . But I swear to Christ, on the grave of me dead mother, that I never touched one, not even to tousle his hair. You see a father with his son, he tosses his kid's hair and 'tis no big deal, but for us, to once . . . to reach out your hand, to let your fingers caress him for just a moment, oh sweet Jaysus, you can't. You do it once, you might never stop.'

A sob escaped him and I wondered if he had, maybe once, done just that. Steel in my voice, I accused him.

'You pig, you did, didn't you? You touched some boy, didn't you?'

Grief racked his frame. The cig tumbled from his mouth, he turned to me, hell in his very eyes, and reached out his hand. I snapped,

'Don't ever think about it. I'll take it off from the elbow – I'm not some altar boy.'

His face was all I've ever seen of pure and total suffering, and God knows I've seen it in most guises. He said, no, pleaded,

'Jack, by all that's holy, I might have thought about it, but I never – may I rot in damnation for all eternity if I speak a word of a lie – I never did.'

Now I lit a cig, didn't offer him, kept steel in my voice, asked,

'And?'

'I was cleared. The boy withdrew the allegation, but mud sticks. If the killer is after priests who . . . you know?'

It had to be said, so I said it.

'If he's after paedophiles.'

His head pulled back, as if I'd slapped him, then,

'Yes.'

I began to walk away. He called,

'Will you help, Jack?'

I didn't know.

I didn't even know if I believed him.

7

*'"Och ocon" . . . that's Irish and roughly
translated means, "Woe Is Me".
The song of my life.'*

KB

The altar boy had hidden the priest's ten shillings under his mattress. His mother found it, accused him of stealing. He told her, tried to tell her about what the priest had done. She'd gotten the switch, a long cane cut at the end, and beaten him mercilessly, screaming,

'You ever repeat that, I'll take the head off you, do you hear me?'

Terence Brown, solicitor.

He looked like a ferret with anorexia.

He seemed aware of this and to be daring you to mention it.

I didn't.

His office was situated on Long Walk and you could see the Atlantic from his window. The shriek of seagulls was clearly audible – always makes me want to cry or travel or both. He sat across a large desk from me and I looked round the room, my eyes resting on a wondrous sculpture of a bronze army. It was awesome in its starkness and majesty. He said,

'John Behan.'

I nodded in appreciation. I've never craved material goods. You spend your life as a drunk, cash is the only goal and the real hangover cure. He shuffled some papers on his desk, said,

'We were beginning to think you'd never show.'

I gave him my best smile – it had worked at the security gig.

'I was otherwise detained.'

He leaned back and his leather chair creaked. Least I think it was the chair – if it was his back, he was seriously fucked. He made a tent of his fingers and added *mmmmph* sounds to the gesture. I'm intrigued by that, do they teach it in law school? It's popular with

Bank Managers

Psychiatrists

Garda superintendents.

I'd witnessed it from psychopaths on two occasions. Cleared his throat, said,

'Well, you'll want to know your situation?'

'That'd be great.'

Not the answer he expected but his agenda wasn't high on my list of priorities. He began,

'Mrs Bailey was an extremely shrewd woman. Oddly, she'd no living relatives.'

Permitted himself a small smile, displaying yellow teeth, the gums in galloping recession. It didn't enhance his appeal. Then,

'I suppose she outlived them all. Apart from small legacies to charity, there wasn't any next of kin to give her estate to. This, of course, made probate fairly straightforward.'

I waited, if not patiently, at least with the appearance of it. He said,

'In addition to a sizeable sum of money, she left you a small apartment in Merchant's Road. It's a top-floor unit, very basic, but need I say, a much-sought-after one, in terms of location. If you wish to sell, I can recommend a good firm.'

I stared at him, said,

'I won't be selling.'

Solicitors aren't fond of snap decisions – where's the fee in that? He gave me the tolerant legal smile, said,

'You haven't seen it yet.'

I enjoyed pissing him off, said,

'Give me the keys, I'll rectify that.'

I thought *rectify* might fly his kite. It didn't. He sighed, passed over a set of keys, the address on a large label, asked,

'If you give me your banking details, I'll arrange for the funds to be transferred.'

Pause.

'I take it you *do* have an account?'

You had to love this sanctimonious prick. I gave him the details. He said,

'The property will be put in your name. If you can stop by next week, if your schedule allows, I'll have the paperwork for you to sign.'

That was it.

I knew he took a dim view of me, but hell, what was new in that? We didn't shake hands on my departure. I headed for Mocha Beans, figured I'd have a large cappuccino to celebrate. Maybe order a cherry muffin, shoot, the works. Got in there and yeah, it was jammed. I had to share a table with a middle-aged woman who was engrossed in the *Irish Times*. The headline screamed about more scandal in the Church. Five priests in Dublin were being investigated over allegations of abuse. Every day, new disclosures. The waitress came over, asked in an American accent,

'And how are you doing today, Sir?'

Jesus, beyond cheerful. She'd a name tag: Debbie. I didn't think I'd be using it, decided to forgo the muffin, said,

'Large cappuccino please, no chocolate sprinkle.'

She seemed delighted with my choice, asked,

'Something to go with that? A slice of Danish, fresh from the oven?'

The woman with the paper smiled and I said,

'No, but thanks for the suggestion.'

I thought about Malachy, about the price I'd paid for previous investigations. Did I have what it required to return? I didn't know. A feeling was building in my system and I realized it was shock.

Shock at the prospect of getting back into the game. The adrenalin rush was massive.

The woman put her paper aside, asked,

'Are you on holiday?'

'No, I'm from Galway.'

She thought about that, then,

'A real native, somewhat of a rare species.'

We had indeed become a city where being a native was unusual. My coffee came and I sipped it, wondering if I suddenly told this stranger I was fresh out of the laughing academy how cordial she would be. She stood, said,

'You have a good day.'

And was gone.

Should I have made a move on her? The old question, and the answer was, too late.

Later, I went to Merchant's Road to see my new home. The building appealed immediately. Granite front, windows opening out to small balconies. I went in, climbed the stairs and found my door, my place! It consisted of bedroom, sitting room, kitchen, all on the small scale. High ceiling, which adds the illusion of space. There was furniture, old but solid, a bed, and in the presses, crockery. It felt like it had never been inhabited, as if it was simply waiting. I opened the windows and gave silent benediction to Mrs Bailey.

I had been to the cinema to see *Goodbye, Berlin*, got a takeaway kebab and had turned into the alleyway leading to the Granary. My mind was see-sawing twixt joy from the magical movie and the loneliness of buying one ticket. Few things emphasize aloneness like the cinema. It's designed for company – they even have *love seats* . . . fuck.

The cashier had asked,

'How many?'

The sad refrain,

'One.'

My answer seemed to echo in the foyer, bounce against the coming attractions and highlight the groups of people in animated conversation. At the next desk, the assistant was selling tickets as fast as he could punch them. *Terminator 3* . . . maybe Arnie's declaration that he'd run for Governor of California was swelling the appeal. The refreshment kiosk was jammed – mega buckets of popcorn and huge cokes. I walked by.

So when the guy came out of the darkened doorway of my apartment, I nearly dropped my kebab. He said,

'Gimme money.'

I muttered,

'Sure.'

Moved the kebab to my left hand, shot out with the right. The second guy would have taken me easily – I'd never considered two. Before he could strike, someone came running down the alley, hit him with a shoulder. I turned, trying to get a handle on what the hell was happening. A man in his early twenties, dressed in a tracksuit, stood over the guy he'd knocked down. He asked,

'Should I kick him in the gut?'

'I would.'

He did.

I asked,

'Who the blazes are you?'

The would-be muggers were moaning and I suddenly noticed their shoes – the heavy black jobs. Only one gang in the world wore those. The Guards. The man said,

'I'm Cody.'

I shook my head. This was supposed to mean something? I asked,

'Want to share a kebab?'

His smile revealed glittering white teeth as he said,

'Man, I love to eat.'

And all the time, I was asking meself,

'Why would the Guards want to rough me up except to warn me off?'

When we got to the flat, he whistled in appreciation, said,

'What a pad.'

He had an American accent, but I'm Irish, I could hear the lilt beneath. His delivery was good but bogus. I got some plates, cut the kebab in two, asked,

'What to drink?'

He was standing at the window, staring at that view, went,

'Bourbon, rocks, beer chaser.'

I smiled, he sounded so close to the real thing. I said,

'I've got tea, water, coffee.'

'Tea's cool.'

While the kettle boiled, I appraised him. Tall with an athlete's build. When he turned towards me his face was solid: brown eyes, straight nose, but the mouth let the picture sag. Thin lips that seemed like an afterthought. Blond hair in the mocked style of the eighties known as a Mullet. He obviously hadn't heard the jokes and derision, or maybe he had, didn't care. I put the plates down and he sat, went,

'You handle yourself well for an old guy.'

I let that slide. What was I going to do, argue the toss? What it did, apart from depress the shit out of me, was make me conscious of my limp. The guy probably figured I had a walking stick, but he'd saved my ass, no question

– the second mugger I'd never even considered. He'd have had me, as the English say, 'Bang to rights.' I owed him, said,

'I owe you.'

He grabbed his portion of the kebab, took a hefty bite, chewed with his mouth open – not a pretty sight but, like I said, I was in his debt. He waved his hand, answered,

'No biggie, dude.'

Dude . . . Jesus.

I sat opposite him, felt a tremor along my spine, knew my hands would shake. He noticed, said,

'All shook up, yeah?'

I didn't think it required a reply. He nodded, said,

'A shot of something, get you squared away.'

It would certainly get me put away. Man, I'd have sold my soul for a Bushmills, Jameson, get that fake warmth to light my guts. He added,

'You can't, huh?'

The old anger surfaced. I went,

'What's that mean?'

He was unfazed, still chewing, raised his left hand in the drinking motion then rolled his eyes, said,

'One's not enough, eh . . . is that how it goes?'

The sheer insanity of alcoholism. If there'd been a bottle in the apartment, I'd have had a large one then put him through the window. I reined in, tried,

'Lucky for me you were passing.'

He raised his eyebrows, echoed,

'Lucky? Luck had nothing to do with it.'

I didn't understand, said,

'I don't understand.'

'I was following you, Jack.'

My name. Did I give it? No, definitely not. He indicated my half of the kebab, asked,

'You gonna chow down? . . . like, I'd hate to see it go begging.'

I stood, pushed the food to him, asked,

'You skip breakfast, that it?'

Then aiming for calm, keeping it low, asked,

'Why are you following me?'

He'd launched into the food and, startling us both, I shouted,

'Leave the fucking food alone.'

He threw his hands up in mock surrender, said,

'Whoah! Take it easy, big guy, take a chill pill. You don't want to get a heart attack. Jeez, bring it down a notch.'

While he was saying this, I considered launching myself across the table, ramming the bloody kebab down his throat. I leaned on the table, said,

'Cody or whatever the hell your name is, listen up. Who the hell are you, why are you following me and how do you know my name? Think you can answer those?'

My cigs were on the table. He flipped open the pack, took out a Zippo, fired up, said,

'I'm trying to cut back, but after vittles you just gotta have that nicotine buzz.'

Saw my expression, grinned, went,

'Okey dokey, 'fess-up time. Hombre, I'm your biggest fan, been reading up on you.' Paused, as if searching for the right words. 'How does it go . . . "I like the cut of your gib"?

In other words, Jack, I want to be a private eye. I want to be your partner. What do you say, want to buddy up?'

I stared at him for a moment, then burst out laughing. Cody didn't like being laughed at, protested,

'I'm serious, dude. I've been following your career. We hook up, we'd clean up.'

Nice pithy slogan, we could put it on a T-shirt. I asked, 'Tell me who you are, and tell me now.'

My tone implied the violence that lingered barely under the surface of every waking hour.

He got it.

Sitting up straight, he wiped his mouth, went,

'OK. I'm like you, Jack. A younger version, but definitely you. I grew up a few streets from where you were raised and in the same shitty poverty. The best cutlery is the only cutlery, am I right?'

I was still chewing on *younger*. You hit your fifties, your bad fifties, and someone brings up age you brace yourself for the onslaught. Whatever they have to say, you know from gut level, complimentary it won't be.

He continued,

'And see, like you, I love books, man. I read all the time – crime, right? I have two hundred books on crime and I'm going to read them all. And oh, yeah, I feed the swans. I applied to be a Guard and they turned me down.'

His face dissolved into misery. I snapped,

'Why?'

'Why do I feed the swans?'

Fuck, this was like pulling teeth, very stubborn teeth. I sighed, said,

'No, why did they turn you down for the Guards?'

His face lit up again. He said,

'I have a bad leg, me left one, hurt it playing sport, and isn't that weird, you got your . . . am . . .'

'Limp.'

'Am, right, your . . . injury from a hurley. Isn't that serendipity?'

It was shite is what I thought. He went on,

'I didn't do very well at school. I don't do authority, and your dad, he knew mine, they were on the Church Sodality together.'

Now I had him, said,

'Wrong guy, buddy. My father, he never served on committees, especially Church ones. If you'd said my mother, you'd have been nearer the mark – she lived in the bloody place, should have been a nun.'

I could feel the old bitterness, the old resentment of her, like bile in my throat. He digested this, then continued,

'I think he knew him, anyway. So with all we have in common, I think we should work together.'

'And this would work, how?'

He was on his feet, pacing, excitement in his whole body.

'I'd handle the field work and you could, like . . .'

He tried to find the right word so I prompted,

'Sleuth?'

'What?'

'To sleuth: to search for clues.'

He suspected I was mocking him, but went with it, uncertainty in his eyes.

'Am, yes, the strategy and stuff. I'm, as you've seen, a hands-on kind of guy.'

He was so earnest I decided not to sling his ass out, said, 'Why not?'

He couldn't believe it, was actually lost for words. I said,

'I'm going to be moving into a new . . . pad . . . in Merchant's Road – you can report to me there. Meanwhile, here's your . . . am . . . assignment.'

He looked round the place, asked,

'You're letting this go?'

'Too conspicuous. Don't want to draw too much attention to ourselves.'

He loved that *ourselves*, went,

'Gotcha.'

Then, as if he'd rehearsed, plunged,

'I won't need paying right off. Like, I'll do it . . .'

'Pro bono.'

'Pro what?'

My leg was aching, I wanted to lie down.

'Here's what I want you to do.'

He was all attention, his forehead scrunched.

'There's a group of winos at the Square, they're based near the automatic toilets . . .'

He leaped in,

'I know them. You want me to go undercover, infiltrate them. I won't shave, I'll—'

'Shut up.'

Like hitting a puppy. He looked so wounded, I said,

'The first thing you got to do is learn to listen. Are you listening?'

He nodded miserably. Where did I get this shit? I continued,

'There's a guy – long grey hair in a ponytail, name of Jeff – he sits a little apart from the main cluster. I want you to find out how he's doing and – here's the tricky bit – to see how you can get him off the street.'

He wanted to ask a ton of questions, but I was in, asked,

'You think you can handle that?'

'Yeah, boss.'

'OK, you got a phone number?'

He had a mobile and a land line. Cautioned about the land line as it was his parents' home. I was afraid to ask if he still lived there. At least he didn't have a business card, but it could only be a matter of time. As he prepared to leave, he suddenly hugged me. Truly, I was losing my grip, never anticipated it. He said,

'We're going to make some team.'

I didn't doubt that for a minute.

My dreams were vivid, a macabre blend of kebabs, headless priests, a church without candles and a cemetery with pints of Guinness on the graves. I came to, gasping, covered in sweat, muttered,

'Jesus.'

And dragged myself to the shower. Got it scalding, as if steam could erase the memories. I had no appetite but forced down some dry toast, got some coffee brewing. I didn't want a cig but lit one anyway. Addiction wakes before you do, impatiently waiting, going 'I've *torture* on hold for you.'

I had some serious thinking to do. The whole Cody deal

stank to high heaven. As I replayed it, the thought struck me,

'What if . . . Jesus, what if he set up the muggers, the whole scene was planned, he's in cahoots with the Guards?'

Then of course I'd be grateful, as I had been, and would agree to most anything he asked, like him being my partner. I'd never done the buddy gig. Lone wolf was my calling. And I had to ask meself, why did I agree? . . . apart from gratitude. Was it boredom? Just not giving a toss? . . . I truly didn't know.

I did know he wasn't what he seemed, the act of naive kid didn't play. But I decided to let it run, else how would I discover his agenda? Keep your friends close and your enemies closer still, wasn't that the line? He wasn't my friend, that was for sure. If he was an enemy, I'd know soon enough.

Then I figured, what the hell? If nothing else, it was going to be interesting.

That figuring would very nearly be the death of me.

8

*'Fathers are afraid that their children's natural
love may be eradicated.'*

Pascal, *Pensées*, 93

Turned on the radio, blast the silence. The news. A Vatican document was discovered by a Texan lawyer. Published in Latin, he called it a blueprint for deception and concealment. Sixty-nine pages, with the seal of Pope John XXIII, in 1962 it was sent to every bishop in the world.

Some postage.

It contained guidelines for bishops to deal discreetly with victims of abuse. Irish bishops were told to follow a policy of strictest secrecy. Excommunication was threatened if they spoke out. Victims, after making a complaint, were to take an oath of secrecy.

I got dressed, went out. My limp was pronounced – going down three flights of stairs didn't help. At a shop across the street, I bought the papers and the woman said,

'Nice morning for it.'

I hadn't the energy to ask what, lest she tell me. Back up the stairs, I settled in the chair by the window and began to read. The Vatican revelations were front-page news. The Vatican document, called *Crimine Solicitationes* – instructions on proceeding in cases of solicitation – dealt with

84

sexual abuse between a priest and a member of his congregation in the confessional.

I stopped reading, went and brewed some fresh coffee, thinking how Father Joyce had been beheaded in the confessional. The rage it required to sever the head would have to be ferocious. A shudder passed through me.

I returned reluctantly to the papers.

The document also covered 'the worst crime of all', which it described as an obscene act by a cleric with 'youths of either sex'.

Was the killer out there, reading this?

The description *youths* tore at my guts, but worse was to follow. The next few words made me retch.

'. . . or with brute animals (Bestiality).'

The bishops were instructed to pursue these cases in 'the most sensitive way . . . restrained by a perpetual silence . . . And everyone is to observe the strictest secrecy which is commonly regarded as a secret of the Holy Office.'

In May 2001, the Vatican sent a letter to bishops, clearly stating that the 1962 instruction was still in force.

I put the papers aside, darkness all around me. The phone rang and I jumped. The heart sideways in me, I grabbed the receiver, went,

'Yeah?'

'Jack Taylor, it's Ni Iomaire.'

'Ridge.'

I didn't hear her customary annoyance when I used the English version of her name. I asked,

'What's up?'

'Can we meet? I need to talk to you.'

'Sure. You OK?'

'I don't know.'

Then I recognized the tone in her voice, something I'd never heard in her – fear. I asked,

'Did something happen?'

'I'll be in the Southern at noon. Will you come?'

'Sure, I—'

Click.

The Great Southern Hotel, situated at the bottom of Eyre Square, had been closed for six months' renovation. I'd known the doorman more years than either of us would admit. He had the red face, broken veins of the daily heavy drinker. But he managed to stay employed and that was a whole lot more than I'd ever achieved. He gave me the Galway greeting.

'How's it going, Jack?'

In all our years, we'd never pinned down that elusive *it*. Perhaps it was all-encompassing. I did my part, said,

'It's going good.'

He spread his arms out, indicating the changes, asked,

'What do you think?'

I didn't think much, it looked exactly the same, said,

'They did a great job.'

He beamed, as if he personally had overseen the work. In Ireland, we're never slow to take the credit where it isn't due. We call it honesty. Doormen, cab-drivers, barmen, they're the best source of information. I leaned close to get that conspiracy angle going, said,

'Bad business about Father Joyce.'

His eyes lit up. Scandal . . . near as good as a hidden half of Jameson. He said,

'He used to come here, you know.'

I kept my face grave, prompted,

'You'd have known him then?'

About as dumb an observation as you can make, but it was the right track. Animated, he took my arm, moved me away from the door, said,

'Every Friday, five o' clock, you could set your watch, he'd be in.'

He shot out his right hand, finger to the far corner.

'Always the same table and a large Paddy, pint of Guinness. Some Americans were in his place once. I shunted them.'

He stared at me, awaiting the verdict on his action. I said,

'Good one.'

I got a few notes, palmed them to him, asking,

'Where did he go during the renovations?'

He looked at me as if I was mad, said,

'How the hell would I know?'

And stomped off.

What had I learned? Precious little. Sat in the corner myself, wished I could have the Paddy and chaser. Ordered a pot of coffee and watched the door. Half an hour before Ridge appeared. She arrived, wearing a white T-shirt, tan jeans, sandals, the outfit declaring,

'Hey, I'm cool, not a thing bothering me.'

Her face told a different tale – lines of worry along her forehead, her mouth a grim purse. I stood as she approached but the gesture didn't impress her. She sat, said,

'I got caught in traffic.'

I indicated the coffee pot, said,

'It's cold, I can order fresh . . .'

She shook her head, did what police do – checked the exits, windows, number of people. You do it automatically and it never goes away. She said,

'I ever tell you I was thinking of being a nurse? I'd applied to the Guards, but if they turned me down, then nursing was my next choice.'

The way she said it, you'd think we had frequent intimate chats. We certainly had a lot of mileage, but never by choice. I said,

'No, you didn't tell me.'

She was fiddling with the strap of her watch, the only sign of her agitation. She said,

'As preparation, I was working as Care Assistant with old people. One old woman, lived in Rossaville, she was very wealthy but a cow, a walking bitch.'

The vehemence of her words was fevered. It was like Ridge was back there, with the woman. I wanted to shout,

'Go for it, girl! Get it out, vent that fucker.'

She said,

'The day I got accepted for the Guards and had a date to report for training, I went to tell the old biddy I wouldn't be seeing her any more. She wouldn't hear of it. You know what she said?'

I'd no idea and shook my head.

'You're being paid to care for me.'

Ridge almost smiled at the memory, said,

'I told her, the cheque's not been written that would make me care for you.'

I wondered how this related to what was spooking her. She said, as if reading my mind,

'That's nothing to do with why I wanted to talk to you.'

I must have looked confused. I'd been trying for *attentive* and she added,

'I wanted you to understand that being a Guard is what I do care about. Sometimes I think it's all I have.'

As if I needed that spelled out. The day I got kicked off the Force was among the darkest of my life. You hear people say, 'What I do is not who I am.' They were never cops. The rate of suicide among retired cops is through the roof, because you can't stop being one. Everything for me related to my time as a Guard. I never recovered from losing it. All the disasters, one way or another, they'd their basis in that loss. I said,

'I understand.'

I waited, figuring she'd get to it in her own time. Then, 'I'm being stalked.'

I hadn't known what to expect, but this threw me. Took me a few minutes to get my head round it, then I said,

'Tell me.'

Her face was scrunched, her eyes almost closed, the effort of articulating it requiring massive effort. She said,

'The past few weeks, I'd the sense of being watched. Then late-night calls, no one there and when I hit 1471 got blocked call. My apartment – someone's been in there. Nothing taken, just a very subtle rearranging of things. Then yesterday, this came.'

She reached in her jeans, took out a folded envelope. I looked at it – it had her name and address on (in Irish), posted in Galway the day before. I took out a single sheet of paper, read

Say
Your
Prayers
Bitch.

Nothing else.
And the first thought that struck me was,
'Cody?'
Would he be double fucking, me and Ridge?

9

*'Atheism indicates strength of mind,
but only up to a certain point.'*

Pascal, *Pensées*, 225

July 1968, Australian Catholic Record
Father W. Dunphy

It would be extremely foolish to deny that many priests, maybe even the majority of them, young and old, are greatly disturbed with regard to their position in the Church. The priest feels he is no longer in command. His one-time social pre-eminence among his flock has lost no small part of its sheen.

I peered closely at the envelope but it told me nothing. I asked,

'Any idea who it could be?'

She shook her head. I was tempted to say,

'I'll have my colleague look into it.'

But she was too rattled for levity. I didn't know what she thought an ex-drunk, fresh out of the loony bin, could do. I didn't say this either, went with,

'How about if I keep an eye on your home for a few days, see who shows up?'

She turned to look at me, asked,

'Are you up to that? It's like returning to your old job and that's caused you major trauma.'

No argument there, so I tried,

'All I'll do is watch. I get a lead on somebody, I tell you, you take it from there.'

'You fucking bet I will.'

The ferocity stunned us both. Ridge, no stranger to temper, rarely resorted to obscenity and she put her hand to her mouth as if to staunch further outpourings, said,

'I don't like being scared.'

I nearly laughed but reined it in, asked,

'Come on, Ridge, who does?'

She lifted the coffee pot, shook it, then poured some into a cup, swirled it round and put the cup back on the table.

'You have any idea how it is for me, a woman in the Guards? They give out all this positive PR about us being an integral part. The truth is, they don't ever see us bringing a hurley into a dark alley with a suspect, solving it "the old-fashioned way".'

Having been both the recipient of the hurley and the one who wielded it, in alleys and elsewhere, I asked,

'That it, what you want? Get some thug in a lane, give him the lesson of the hurley?'

She didn't bother replying, continued,

'And being gay, don't even go there. I have to fight that discrimination every single day – the Ban Garda are worse than the men. But it's who I am, what I want to do. If I'm scared from outside, I'll never be able to continue.'

I didn't feel a comment on her sexuality would be welcome, so asked,

'What makes you so sure the threats come from outside?'
She looked at me with horror, said,
'Oh no, I couldn't deal with that. It has to be from outside the force, do you hear me? It can't be a Guard.'
I let that go, said with a confidence I didn't believe,
'I'll sort it.'
When she jumped into agreeing with me, I added,
'Anyway, who else have you got?'
Figuring it wouldn't hurt to have a little reciprocation, I took out the sheet of paper with the three names Father Malachy had given me, laid it on the table, asked,
'Can you do background on these guys for me?'
She picked up the list, disbelief on her face, went,
'You can't be – you're working something.'
I kept my face neutral, insisted,
'No, no, I promised a friend of mine I'd have them checked out, it's an insurance gig.'
She wasn't buying it, said,
'You're in no shape for this.'
I put out my hand for the list, snapped,
'Fine, forget it.'
She folded the paper, said,
'I'll see what I can do.'
To get past the moment, I told her about Mrs Bailey, the legacy, the place on Merchant's Road. She allowed herself a small smile, said,
'You deserve some luck.'
Surprised me, it was as close to warmth as she'd ever come.
'I'm glad you're pleased.'

She was standing, ready to leave, and I felt our relationship might finally have inched forward. She said,

'I didn't say I was pleased, I said you deserved it. God knows, you never earned it.'

As I said . . . *inching* forward.

Ridge had a house rented in Palmyra Park, en route to Salthill. I didn't know how I could watch the house unobserved. If I sat in a car, sooner or later someone would call the Guards. Planting myself on the street was out of the question. There was a house directly opposite with a B&B sign. Decided to take a chance, rang the doorbell. The woman who answered was in her sixties, friendly and homely. I'd dressed to impress – blazer, white shirt, tie – said I'd be in town for a week, any vacancies?

She said,

'God sent you.'

Which seemed an exaggeration, but definitely in my favour. I asked,

'Busy?'

She raised her eyes to heaven, said,

'Once the races are over, we're in quare street.'

The Irish pronounce *queer* as *quare* and it's not anything to do with Gay issues, it's purely for the sound of the word, to give it a full and resounding flavour. We love to taste the vocabulary, swill it around the mouth, let it blossom out into full bloom.

I did the smart thing, got out my wallet, laid a wedge in her hands, said,

'Would it be possible to have a room overlooking the street?'

She was staring at the money, said,

'You can have any room you like, we haven't had a sinner since Sunday.'

The tricky part. I tried,

'I'll be in my room a lot. I'm compiling a guide for the Tourist Board, so lots of paperwork. Some days I'll be travelling and my assistant will be here, a young man, very presentable.'

She didn't have a problem with this, asked about meals. I said a kettle would answer all our needs. Her name was Mrs Tyrell, she was a widow, and her daughter Mary helped with the B&B in addition to attending college. Then she rolled her eyes, said Mary was studying Arts, exclaimed,

'*Arts* . . . I wanted her to do Science, they're crying out for them, but devil a bit of notice she pays. Fellas and pubs, that's what she cares about. Pity they don't give a degree in that.'

I smiled and she asked,

'When can I expect you?'

'Monday, how would that be?'

That would be fine, she agreed. We shook hands and I was out of there. I now found myself in the surreal position of having three homes, how mad does it get? Come out of the madhouse and live in three places – it made a kind of demented sense, didn't it?

I walked towards the prom, easing the pain from my limp as I moved. Stopped for a moment, not crediting what I was seeing. Two Guards on mountain bikes! With safety helmets, leggings, the whole outdoor kit. An elderly woman had also stopped, said,

'Will you look at the cut of them?'

She must have been seventy, with that permed hair they provide with your pension and wide blue eyes that age had deepened. Her accent was the pure Galwegian you rarely hear any more. A blend of sense and mischief, the hard edge loosened by the speed of the vowels, she made me yearn for a childhood I never had. I asked, keeping it local,

'When did they start this crack?'

She watched them turn at Grattan Road, zip down towards Claddagh, said,

'Ary, a few months ago. It was in the papers, how bikes would help them tackle crime better.'

'You think it's made any difference?'

It wasn't a serious question, just the Irish oil to keep the conversation cooking. She looked at me as if I was stupid, said,

'Can you see them chasing joyriders? A teenager, mad on cider, in a stolen car, going over a hundred and them bright sparks in pursuit . . . on bikes?'

It was some picture. She added,

'They don't know their arse from their elbow.'

Which is as low as it gets. She was looking more closely at me, asked,

'Do I know you?'

I put out my hand, said,

'Jack Taylor.'

She took my hand in both of hers, asked,

'Didn't your mother just die?'

'She did.'

'Ah, God rest her, she was a saint.'

I tried not to curse. The *saint* label is usually trotted out when you've no idea who the person was. She muttered something I didn't catch. For a dreadful moment, I thought she'd begun a decade of the Rosary, then,

'She's better off out of it.'

I nodded as I hadn't a coherent reply. She said,

'The town is gone to hell. That poor priest, they took the head off him.'

I said it was indeed awful, beyond belief, and trailed off in a cliché about God's mysterious ways. That seemed to jolt her. She repeated,

'Mystery . . . There's no mystery, I know who did it.'

Maybe I'd solve the case right there at a bus stop. I prompted,

'You do?'

'Them non-nationals, bringing voodoo and heathen rituals into a decent country.'

'Oh.'

A bus was approaching and she flagged it, said,

'Mark my words, you'll find a black fella did it.'

As she got on the bus, she added,

'I'll say a prayer for your mother, the poor creature. None of us safe in our beds . . .'

Guards on bikes. When I was a child, Galway was more a village than a town. Certainly in its mentality. There was a Guard, Hannon, who'd patrol our area, he had a bike with an actual basket. He'd do his shopping, then spin around the streets, stop, have a chat with somebody. He'd be perched on the bike, one leg on the path as ballast, clips to the ends of his pants to prevent them from catching.

Crime was very low key – a murder would get national headlines for weeks. Now they can't keep pace with the numbers.

The priest also had a bike, he'd use it when collecting the parish dues. His word was law, he'd more power than any Guard. Who could have foretold the massive fall from grace?

I walked on to Salthill, the heat increasing. Europe was suffering from impossibly high temperatures and we were getting the tail end of it. Passed a young woman dressed in shorts and singlet. Her skin was red as a lobster, I could already see blisters forming. I wanted to suggest she cover up but she caught my look, glared at me. I said nothing.

Salthill was packed, ice-cream vendors making a huge profit. A and E departments were urging people to be careful and staff were already overrun with cases of sunstroke. Telling people in Ireland to be wary of the sun was as alien as bacon without cabbage. Lots of men in the Irish fashion for hot weather: baggy shorts, white legs and sandals. Worse, if such were possible, sandals with thick woollen socks.

Standing over the beach, I saw acres of white and whiter flesh, skin that seemed never to have experienced the sun. I was seized with the compulsion to drink a cold pint of lager, beads of moisture clinging to the rim, bubbles dancing along the side. Two, three, I'd hammer them and the following ten minutes would be relief beyond under-standing. I turned and headed back to town, sweat drenching my shirt.

The rest of the day I spent in a frenzy of activity. Bought

chairs, table, bookcase, electric kettle, blankets, sheets, and had them delivered. Arranged for a phone and electricity. Met one of the neighbours, who asked,

'Are you moving in?'

He looked as if he couldn't believe his eyes. I said,

'Yes.'

He took a deep and yes, angry, breath, said,

'This is a quiet house.'

And was gone before I could wallop him. What? I looked like a party animal? Fuck him.

Nine in the evening, I was near moved in. The phone was set, I had the furniture and, best of all, I didn't have a drink. Rang Cody, arranged to meet him the next morning. I spent the night in the Granary, stayed away from the window – that view was lodged in my soul, I couldn't bear to watch it for one last time. In bed at ten, knackered, and my dreams involved lager-swilling priests on bikes.

When I woke, I packed my few things, went out the door and, in true macho pose, didn't look back, not once.

10

'Contradiction: contempt for our existence, dying for nothing, hatred of our existence.'

Pascal, *Pensées*, 157

'Jeff is gone.'

I was meeting with Cody in the new coffee bar at Jury's. They'd a menu of designer blends on display. Cody was wearing a bright tan leather jacket with a T-shirt proclaiming

We rock.

His hair was awash with gel and his opening remark was the above. Before I could reply, he said,

'He hasn't been seen for five days. Though he was part of the drinking school, he didn't really belong.'

I wanted to ask who did, but he continued,

'I checked the Simon Community, the hospitals, even the morgue, but no trace of him. That pub he owned, Nestor's, is up for sale. A guy working there hasn't seen your friend for months.'

Your friend – that burned. Whatever else, I hadn't been much of that. Cody added,

'The wife, Cathy . . . is in Galway . . .'

He let that hang there to see how I'd respond, and when I didn't, he continued,

'I spread some money around the drinking school, left my phone number, said there'd be more if they had any news.'

He considered this, then,

'But homeless people, drinkers, they're not going to have a huge concentration span.'

I was impressed at his diligence, how he'd covered all the bases.

'You've done good work.'

He gave a knowing smile, said,

'I was born for this gig.'

The waitress asked what we'd have and Cody said,

'Black coffee, a pot of the stuff, right Jack?'

'Why not?'

He reached in his jacket, produced a business card, handed it to me.

Like this:

Taylor and Cody
Investigations
No divorce work.

And five – count them – phone numbers. On the top right-hand corner was what looked suspiciously like a Sherlock Holmes deerstalker. I hoped not. He was watching my face, couldn't wait, blurted,

'I put your name first, you being the senior operative, and see, the divorce stuff shows we're serious, only primo gigs.'

I hadn't words to match my astonishment.

'You . . . We . . . have five numbers?'

He was shaking his head, going,

'Naw, I only have my mobile, but it looks good and you, you have to get a mobile.'

I began to shove the card back to him. He said,

'No, no, I've another five hundred. That's for you, the very first off the press. This is the moment.'

I was afraid he was going to explain. He did.

'The moment . . . Jack . . . when you stepped up to the base, when what you called *finding* became a pro outfit.'

The coffee came, thank Christ, deferring an opinion from me. Cody gave the girl a radiant smile. At least he hadn't given her a card – not yet – said,

'That'll hit the spot.'

I produced an envelope, handed it over, said,

'You've earned this.'

He took it, put it in his jacket, said,

'I didn't expect a salary yet.'

Yet?

He poured the coffee, raised his cup, toasted,

'Here's looking at you, kid.'

I tried to pretend he hadn't, covered with,

'We have a new case.'

Case.

There, it was out, was that so bad? Oh yeah. Before he could nauseate me with an even worse cliché, I outlined the stalking of Ridge, the B&B we'd be occupying next week. If he'd been glowing before, he was lit up now.

'We're going undercover, I love it! We'll need a camera

and, of course, junk food. Stake-outs are hell, man, you need to maintain a sugar rush.'

Sounding like he'd been on numerous ones. I was afraid to raise the issue, said instead I'd take Monday, Tuesday and he could do the next two days, then we'd review the situation. He was filling his cup again, more caffeine for his already racing system, said,

'Aye aye, skipper.'

I stared at him.

'Cody, you've got to promise me something.'

'Name and claim it, skip.'

'Don't ever call me skipper or any derivative.'

The oddest thing – that night I dreamed that Cody was my son, and I was delighted. When I woke, I could recall the dream in its entirety. Shook me head, asking me own self,

'What's with you?'

Wish-fulfilment?

Not having children is a burden you don't even know you carry. You shrug it off, go 'I'd be a lousy parent,' or mutter about loss of freedom. But somewhere deep in the treacherous human psyche is the ache of loss. The worst kind of pain, to miss something you never had, and worse, never will. The heart wants what it will never hold. Though I'd need a drink to admit it, a lot of drinks, my fear was to end up like the consul in *Under the Volcano*, Lowry's searing depiction of alcoholism at its truest and most ferocious. That after they threw me in the hole, they'd throw a dead dog in after me. That imaginary dead dog had howled through many of my worst nightmares.

Early morning is the time for cold truth and I realized that yes, I saw Cody as a surrogate son, and for that reason alone I was harsh on him. Would never dare let him get close.

The ones I let get close get annihilated.

I recalled Cody asking,

'This woman, Ridge, right? She your main squeeze?'

Oh God, I thought he'd peaked but he seemed to be just warming up. I shook my head, said,

'Not likely.'

He was nodding.

'I'm with you, Jack. We're on the same page, singing from the same hymn sheet.'

Enough already. I snapped,

'What does that mean?'

He raised his right hand, made a gun of his thumb and index finger, dropped the hammer, said,

'You and me, Jack, we're not the tied-down type. I'm not saying we're commitment phobics, but there's a big sea out there, we're going to cast our rods more than once.'

Rods.

I'd have to shoot him. He was a blend of Oprah and Jerry Springer – is there a more awesome hybrid? I reached for the bill, just couldn't take another moment, but he was quick, grabbed it and winked. If I was ever mad enough to go on a *stake-out* with him, I'd swing for him. I decided to act on my instinct, leaned in, asked,

'How do you feel about stalkers?'

If he was guilty, he sure hid it well. He was taken aback though, then sneered,

'The scum of the earth.'

I jabbed a finger in his chest, said,

'You remember you said that.'

Outside, I shook myself, to rid myself physically of the whole meeting. My worst dread was that it might be contagious and I'd begin to talk in a similar fashion. American television had given our young people a bastardized language that dredged up Homer Simpson, Eminem and MTV. *Fear Factor* was one of the most popular programmes in the country, not to mention the rip-offs such as *Joe Millionaire*. The result was a language that primarily set your teeth on edge. Perhaps that was the whole point.

The rest of the day I spent organizing my home. At intervals, it dawned on me I actually owned it. I was finally in the realm, if not of stability, at least of security. I wanted to ring the solicitor, check there hadn't been a mistake, that nothing could go wrong. I rang Ridge, asked,

'Are you at work?'

'Day off.'

She sounded listless so I said,

'Hey, you want some lunch?'

'I'm not hungry.'

Then before I could respond, she said,

'Those three names?'

'Yes?'

'I have some information.'

'Terrific, so . . . you want to have coffee or something?'

No answer, then,

'I'll come to the Granary.'

Whoops.

'Am, I moved.'

More animation in her voice, sarcasm too.

'It wasn't good enough, that it?'

Phew-oh. She was one hard lady to like. When they threw around the description *ball-buster*, I think they'd her in mind. I said,

'I told you I came into some good luck, remember?'

I could hear the sigh in her voice, then,

'Whatever.'

Fuck this, I thought, near shouted,

'You meeting me or what?'

'McSwiggan's, eight o'clock, be on time.'

Click.

My apartment was taking shape. It had the essentials – the only thing missing was books. No matter what I lost, and God knows, I'd lost so much, I somehow always held on to a library of sorts. With my Garda all-weather coat, they were part of my territory, part of who I was.

Or not?

Bookless in Galway.

I hadn't opened a volume in months. The death of the child rendered everything obsolete. For a moment, I felt despair like I seldom ever did, a bleak bone-chilling voice that cajoled,

'Why bother with any of it?'

Got moving, turned on the new TV and wouldn't you know, an ad for Guinness, the pint near perfect in its black-ness, a creamy head of incitement and allure. Two guys at a bar, waffling, the drinks untouched before them. What the hell was the matter with them? Talking . . . when they could be drinking. I was almost shouting, going,

'Drink the bloody stuff.'

And caught myself, said,

'Jeez, get a grip.'

Showered, with the water scalding, to burn the obsession away. As if you could.

Ridge was already in McSwiggan's when I got there. One of those miniature bottles of red wine in front of her. You get exactly a glass and a quarter from it – I know, I measured. Alkies always know the amount a bottle holds – never enough. Like a snooker player, the focus is always on the one to come. What's in front of you is a done deal. I got a coke, sat opposite her, asked,

'Waiting long?'

'Do you care?'

Barbed or what? Jeez, here we went already. I wanted to shout, No, I don't care, but chose to forgo the kick of that, poured half the coke into my glass, tried,

'Slainte.'

'Yeah, yeah.'

She put a sheet of paper on the table. Two names on it.

Tom Reed
4, Shantalla Place
Galway

and

Michael Clare
56, Long Walk
Galway

I asked,

'Where's the third guy?'

She looked at me, said,

'He died five years ago. The remaining two – one supplies bouncers to nightclubs and the other, Michael Clare, he's an engineer. Why are you interested in them? They've no history of crime, appear to be upright citizens. But I don't know, is it coincidence, both single and in their early forties?'

I couldn't resist, went,

'It's Ireland, bachelors are part of the landscape.'

She grimaced, said,

'And usually living with their mothers.'

She had finished the wine. I'd never known her to finish a drink. Usually it was just something to have on the table. I asked,

'Another?'

She jumped up, said,

'I'll get my own.'

And did. Returning, she poured it straight away, took a hefty slug. Before I could stop myself, I said,

'You need to be careful with that stuff.'

She seemed like she might strike me, gathered herself, said,

'This, from you? That's rich. I think I have a distance to travel before I sink to your level.'

Touché!

But I didn't want to let it go, said,

'I'm probably the best person to know. You want to avoid hell, check out the territory with an inmate.'

She raised her glass, defiance writ large, said,

'Cheers.'

I let it slide, said,

'I've put some things in place, to see if we can catch your stalker.'

Enraged, she spat,

'Don't call him that.'

'A stalker? What? Come on, is there some pc term we're supposed to use now?'

She stood up, said,

'*My* stalker. Don't you ever, like ever, call him *mine* . . .'

And she stormed off. I wanted to shout,

'Drink all you like, it's never going to give you a personality.'

There was some wine in the second bottle that would maybe cover the bottom of the glass, give me that tiny lift I craved with all my being. A barmaid, wiping tables, approached, asked,

'These done?'

'Oh yeah.'

11

*'And I go on contradicting him until he understands that
he is a monster that passes all understanding.'*

Pascal, *Pensées*, 420

I decided to go and see Tom Reed first – he was the one who supplied bouncers to nightclubs. Another indication of how Ireland had changed. In my youth, I don't think there was a single bouncer in the country. Now, almost every pub, club, hotel had them. They even had a school. I'm not kidding. Ludicrous as it sounds, there was a year-long course in it. Among the subjects were crowd control and the art of defusing situations. I guess, if all else failed, you could return to basics and kick the living shit out of people. Lest you be confused and believed it was simply an extension of the security business, it was listed under the heading 'Entertainment Enterprises'. When Jan 1st rolled round with the proposed ban on smoking in pubs, clubs, prisons, hospitals, the bouncers were going to need a little more under their jackets than people skills.

I was heading along Mary Street when a Daimler pulled up beside me. I'd been limping along, preparing my approach to Reed. I'd more or less decided not to begin with 'Let's cut the shit, did you behead Father Joyce?'

The front and back doors opened, two very large men got out, blocked my path. I thought,

'Uh-oh.'

Their shoes . . . Guards. You can always tell. Heavy black jobs with the thick soles. Few items as good for the solid kicking. Tried and tested and yet to be found wanting. The first one said,

'Taylor.'

Not a question. The second one glared at me, not liking much what he saw, said,

'Get in the car.'

I looked round, didn't see any likely citizen about to protest. The first one added,

'The superintendent wants a word.'

The devil was in me, urging to ask,

'No chance it might be a civil one?'

Went with,

'It's not real convenient right now.'

The second one smiled, said,

'We won't take much of your precious time.'

Translation: Get in the fucking car.

I did.

The second piled into the back beside me and the driver clocked the mirror, eased out into traffic. The guy beside me was wearing aftershave, a bucket of it. Took me a moment to identify the name . . . then . . . Brut. Jeez, I didn't even know they still made it. Maybe he'd stockpiled it, cornering the market. The early seventies, it was the scent of choice. Came in that distinctive green bottle with a silver medallion and guys lashed it on like a blessing. Women have a hard life but that mass era of Brut must have been among the blackest spots. Then it disappeared.

I looked at his left hand. Wedding band. Perhaps his wife figured it ensured he wouldn't play around. We passed Mill Street and I asked,

'We're not going to the station?'

And no one answered. If they were going to drop me in the Bay, it'd be a relief to escape the Brut. We cruised through Salthill, past Blackrock and turned into the golf club. Pulled to a stop and the guy in the front said,

'Get out.'

I did and the driver said,

'He's waiting in the bar.'

I looked at the guy in the rear, then back to the driver, asked,

'You get hazardous pay?'

A flicker of a smile, then the window rolled up. As a child, I'd been here a few times, searching for golf balls. Usually got chased off. I didn't belong and didn't think I ever would. Went in, past lots of guys in bright sweaters talking loud and saying, *birdy . . . four-ball . . . eagle*, as if the words carried weight. Found the bar, and at a large window table was Clancy. Dressed in a diamond-patterned sweater and, I swear, cravat. Nobody – and I mean nobody – other than Roger Moore and the stray mason wears them. Even Edward Heath had managed to forgo them. John Major had wanted to wear them but lacked the balls.

Clancy had golf pants, those shiny affairs that chafe your thighs and make a swishing noise when you walk. Slip-on cordovans on his feet. His face was ruddy, stout, well fed.

His once full head of hair was now a sweepover, drawing notice to his accelerating baldness. A pot of coffee, one cup before him.

I walked over, feeling like the poor relation whose sole mission is to beg. He stared at me, said,

'Sit down.'

I did.

We had a moment of eyeballing, the macho stuff. Hard to credit we'd been great friends, back in my days as a Guard. I got bounced and he got promoted. An inversion of 'Amazing Grace' unfolded in my head. 'Was found but now am lost.'

Oh yeah.

He said,

'The limp hasn't improved.'

I smiled, thinking,

'Game on.'

Answered,

'Least mine is visible.'

A waiter appeared, asked if the Super required fresh coffee, then looked at me. Clancy said,

'He's not a member.'

They both got a kick out of that. I waited and he reached in his pocket, flicked a card on the table. I could see,

Taylor and Cody
Investigations
No divorce work.

He asked,

'Is that a joke?'

'Not to Cody.'

'You set up in business, you better get a licence.'

'Yes Sir.'

He lifted the coffee pot, poured a cup, added cream, sugar, took a sip, went,

'Ah . . . lovely.'

Then,

'I'm surprised they let you out of the madhouse. Thought we were rid of you.'

I let him have that one. If he wanted to fire the cheap shot, I'd let him blaze. Someone shouted to him from the corridor, ready to tee off. I said,

'Don't let me keep you from your game.'

He prepared to stand, said,

'The priest who was murdered – don't even think of going near that.'

I put up my hands, said,

'Why would I?'

He let out a deep belch, said,

'Listen to me, Taylor, listen good. I know all about you. That lunatic Father Malachy, who was probably shagging your oul wan, they say he's going to enlist your help.'

I wanted to wallop the smug smile off his face, ask him was it true his mother was the town ride? I said,

'If you know so much, how come you don't know Malachy and I have bad history? Not as bad as you and I, but you get the drift.'

He leaned over, a smell of mint on his breath, said,

'As for your security job, you can scratch that. I told them you were a bad risk.'

Watching me to see how that landed, he administered his coup de grâce, the one he'd been holding.

'If your *firm* want to investigate something, put your detection skills to the test, I might have something for you.'

This was going to be bad, but I asked,

'Yeah, what would that be?'

He pulled himself up to his full height, shoulders back – he'd practised this in front of the mirror – said,

'They pulled a wino out of the canal. All we can tell is he was in his fifties. Ring any bells? Maybe you could solve it for us, clear our books, eh?'

My heart pounded. I thought,

'Jeff.'

I tried to keep my voice neutral, asked,

'How do you know he was a wino?'

He took a long moment, then,

'The stench of him.'

Outside, as the Americans say, my ride had gone. I walked down the drive, my head in turmoil, going,

'Oh God, if God there be, let it not be Jeff.'

Spent the rest of the morning trying to find where the body was. Tedious, frustrating, but primarily terrorizing. At four thirty I was in the city morgue, finally allowed to view the corpse. I stood before a metal table, a sheet covering the body, enclosed by the institution-green colour on the walls, dizzy from smells, real and imagined. The attendant, impatient, asked,

'You ready yet?'

A whine in there, but I couldn't really start beating on

him, tempting though it was. I nodded and, like some second-grade magician, with a flourish he whipped off the sheet – this was his party piece.

Closed my eyes real tight and begged, did the old Catholic barter, whispered,

'God, if You let this not be Jeff, I won't smoke again. I give You my word.'

What else did I have? And that item was shaky, suspect, at the best of times. As a child, you wanted something – something impossible, like civility from your mother – you went to the Abbey, lit a candle and did the trade-off. Telling the Sacred Heart, 'If Mum is nice to me, I won't hate people.'

Shit like that.

Never worked. She was hostile till she drew her last bitter breath, which is some achievement. I thought of Jeff, his love of that child, the way his eyes lit up when she smiled. Thought too of his face when he realized the broken tiny body on the footpath was his daughter. And she was lying there, her head twisted to the side, a small pool of blood under her ear, because his best friend, me, wasn't paying attention.

The very first time I met him, the signs in his pub read, NO BUD LIGHT. He was my age, and always wore a waist-coat, black 501s like Springsteen and his long grey hair was tied in a ponytail. I'd been a Guard – it was my training to kick the crap out of men with ponytails. It said so in the manual, under *Section # 791: beat on hippies, students, leftwingers.*

He had effortless cool, the real kind, none of that poised shite. I introduced him to Cathy Bellingham, an ex-punk from London who'd washed up in Galway while kicking a heroin habit. Such was the nature of our cosmopolitan city these days. Who could have foreseen it. She married him, like some Jane Austen novel written by Hunter S. Thompson.

Against all the odds, it worked, and they had the little girl. I loved them and deeply envied them. They had what I could only ever dimly imagine, and I was the one who smashed it to smithereens. Jeff wasn't just my best mate, he was probably my only one.

My hands were clenched tight. I broke the skin on my palm with my nails, and welcomed the tiny throb of pain. The attendant was out of patience, snapped,

'Know him?'

He was chewing a Juicy Fruit, the aroma sickening in its strength. I looked down, took an unsteady breath, must have been silent for nearly five minutes as my mind whirled, then,

I said,

'No. No, I don't.'

He wrapped the gum around his front teeth, said,

'No one ever knows the winos, they're truly the cast away.'

'What happens to him?'

Snapped the gum with a long tongue, said,

'We burn 'em.'

Jesus.

'It used to be a pauper's grave, but the city is running out of land.'

I was seriously angry, said,

'People are so inconsiderate.'
He looked at me with vague interest, asked,
'How's that?'
'Dying . . . using up valuable land.'
He gave a throaty swallow, went,
'That's sarcasm, right?'
'Or something close.'
'No biggie, I get it a lot, it's an outlet for rage.'
I turned to stare at him, asked,
'What, you took psychology?'
He gave a superior grin, said,
'I know people.'
'Well, you sure know dead ones.'
He shrugged, said,
'It's a job, right?'
I made to leave, said,
'Thing is, you're wasted. Guy like you, the caring profes-
sions are crying out for you.'
As I was leaving, he shouted,
'Have one for me.'
'What?'
'You're going for a drink, right?'
Before I could answer, he said,
'The pub across the road? Saddest freaking place in the
country. It's where the relatives go . . . Man, not a whole
lot of music there, you need a lively joint.'
'And why would I need that?'
He gave me the look, the silent *duh*, then,
'You lucked out. The stiff – you didn't know him.'
Stiff.

I seriously wanted to pound on this guy, to quote my mother: *You'd never tire beating him.* I said,

'You call that lucking out?'

He shrugged. I'm never taken by that gesture, convinced they rehearse it, get the lift exactly so. He said,

'You're a funny guy.'

I couldn't resist, said,

'You should catch me on a good day.'

Outside, my whole body sagged. I hadn't realized how tight I'd been wound. That pub was almost directly across. I hoped I'd never discover which arrived first, the morgue or the pub. A whole slice of the Irish psyche in the answer. I'd made me deal with God and He'd delivered, so I couldn't have a drink, not yet . . . Jesus, not now.

I moved on, trying not to look over my shoulder. Passed the Age Concern shop and, to distract myself, went in. Almost in a trance, I picked up a Discman. I'd come late to CDs and iPods were forever to be a mystery. Bought it and the girl said,

'Don't forget the headphones.'

'Oh, right.'

She couldn't have been twenty years old, yet she had natural compassion, an openness that stabbed at my heart. Then, to add to my consternation, she said,

'I'll bet you haven't batteries. You get home and isn't it a devil, none.'

She glanced round at the customers, then slipped two batteries across the counter. I'd swear she winked, but I think I only hoped so. I said,

'You've a lovely nature.'

She wasn't buying, said,

'Get away our that. You should see me at home, I'm a holy terror.'

Do such brief encounters balance the daily awfulness of life? That's too tough a measure, maybe, but for the fleeting moment you have the spur to continue.

I hadn't listened to music in a long, long time. You need a soul for that. Mine withered when the child went out the window. Jeff's too, it seemed. I walked up to Shop Street, went into Zhivago. Declan McEntee was still there, went,

'Good God, it's the resurrection.'

Like I was in the mood for this. He read my expression, said,

'You'll want Johnny Duhan as usual?'

'I have all of his.'

I looked round, saw new releases, and there . . . Emmylou Harris, Warren Zevon. Took both.

Declan said, tapping the Zevon,

'Died two weeks ago.'

'What?'

'Yes, recorded this album knowing he'd only a brief time. Makes it real hard to listen to.'

As he wrapped them, he said,

'Johnny Cash's gone too.'

Christ, I'd have to catch up, start reading the papers or watching the news or something.

Declan gave me the change, asked,

'You all right? You're very quiet.'

And I said,

'At home, I'm a holy terror.'

Robert Palmer died the next day – they were dropping like flies. He didn't have a new album. If I wanted to seriously burn, I could always listen to Johnny Cash with 'Hurt'.

I was burning out.

12

*'We run heedlessly into the abyss, after putting something
in front of us to prevent us seeing it.'*

Pascal, *Pensées*, 183

27 July 2003, Ireland on Sunday

'If he did fire 1,000 bullets at a cost of around fifty cents each, it was a small price to pay for a man who has put so much into the force.'

A colleague of departing Garda Commissioner Pat Byrne, who celebrated his retirement on the Phoenix Park indoor firing range.

Sister Mary Joseph was finally beginning to relax. No one had been apprehended for the murder of Father Joyce and no one had come to ask her any questions . . . she dared to hope that her prayers had been answered. It looked like whoever had murdered the poor man was not coming after her. Anyway, she told herself over and over, she had done nothing wrong, but in her heart she knew she had allowed those boys to continue being abused. No matter how many rosaries she said, and no matter how many rationalizations she made, the voice in her head refused to cease its refrain . . . *You knew, you knew those poor creatures were being horribly abused and you did nothing. It's a sin of omission, you are as guilty as Father Joyce is.*

But most days, she took shameful comfort in the fact that she hadn't been found out, no one was accusing her of anything. One boy had begged her, tears streaming down his face, for help. First she had tried to bribe him with chocolate, but he had had an extreme reaction on seeing it, went deathly pale, looked like he was about to faint, and she had read him the riot act, and, God forgive her, she had boxed his ears. She could still see his little face and hear the awful words, *My bum is bleeding.*

Out loud she intoned, 'Oh, Holy Mother of God, deliver me from this torment.' The boy had begun to inhabit her dreams, except now his tears were tears of blood.

Her hair had begun to fall out and she was hoping that this might be penance enough. Apart from Jesus, the only love of her life had been her father and she dreaded to think he'd be ashamed of her. She fell to her knees, began *Ar n-athair . . .* (Our Father . . .)

I rang Joe Ryan, a guy I knew from my days as a Guard. He worked as a journalist and, while we were cordial when we met, we weren't friends or anything in the vicinity. He answered on the second ring and I went through the usual semi-cordial shite till he cut to the chase, went,

'So, what do you want?'

I faked some offence and he said,

'Cut the bollocks, what do you want?'

I sighed, asked,

'You know of a kid named Cody? In his twenties, has a quasi-American accent and—'

He cut me off. If you lived in Galway and had been here any length of time, Joe knew you. He said,

'All the kids have those accents and yeah, I know him, he's Liam Farraher's son. Why?'

He was a journalist so I decided to confuse him with the truth, said,

'He wants to be my partner in the – are you ready for this? – the private-eye game.'

I could hear him laughing, then he said,

'That's Liam's kid, all right. He's not a bad lad, but – what's the current buzz word? – finding himself.'

I let the obvious pun of finding hang there a bit, and then asked,

'Is he OK? I mean, apart from deluded.'

More laughter, then,

'He worked in computers and was pretty damn good, from what I hear, but he obviously wants to lead an exciting life and so has hooked up with you.'

I let that slide and finally asked,

'I don't need to worry about him then, he's not a nutter or anything?'

He waited a time, then,

'Way I see it, they're in their twenties, they're all deranged.'

What I really wanted to ask was, could I trust him? I went,

'Can I trust him?'

He laughed again, said,

'Jeez, Jack, you have a way of putting things, you know that? Take a look round you. This is the new Ireland, no one believes in the Government or the Clergy, and as for the banks, forget it, they're robbing us blind and admitting it. The only item people trust is money – greed is the new spirituality. You want someone to trust, find yourself a nice puppy and beat the bejaysus out of him. He won't like you, but you'll certainly be able to trust him.'

With all me cynicism, all the lies and treachery I'd encountered, this onslaught caught me blindside. The casual ferocity, the simple dismissal of a whole nation, and hey, this was my gig, I was the one who was bitter. I protested,

'That's a little harsh, don't you think?'

He was laughing full now.

'We're fucked, Jack. We talk like quasi-Americans, we're eating ourselves into obesity, drinking our lights out and abusing our children left, right and centre. The only religion now is *Feather thy own nest*, so if you want to know can you trust some kid, let me put it this way – let him do the donkey work and if he's shite, fire his arse. It's the new dynamic, and lemme go American too . . . Get with the game, buddy.'

He took a deep breath then fired his final salvo right at my most vulnerable spot.

'What's your beef? It's not like he's *your* son.'

Then he hung up – no goodbye or take care or the old Irish-ism, *Mind how you go*.

I guess it was the new dynamic.

I didn't know if this helped or not. Did it? Opted for the cynicism on Cody. Decided I'd let him run another mile or so. I could always fire his arse, or should that be *ass*?

Yet another bad decision on my part.

I began the stake-out on Ridge's home on Monday. Days of numbing boredom. At first, the landlady kept checking on me. A knock at the door, did I need anything – tea, coffee, the paper?

After the third time, I answered with an abrupt,

'What?'

She let me be. The daughter, Mary, the student, was introduced on Tuesday. A looker, with long auburn hair, she had all the confidence of the new Ireland, 100 per cent assurance and little ability. She asked,

'And you're doing exactly what?'

She could have a fine career in the Guards. I gave her the lame story. She didn't believe a word of it, said,

'Sounds very odd to me.'

But her mother intervened, mindful of the week's money she'd had up front, said,

'Now, Mary, leave Mr Taylor alone.'

Reluctantly she did, but giving me a look which warned,

'I'll be watching you.'

I was tempted to mention Sting, but let it slide. I'd been to Charly Byrnes, reconnected with Vinny and bought six books. They stood unread on the table, the light from the window throwing a shadow across the covers. You figure with a watching gig, you'll have tons of time to read. Never opened a single volume. The art of sitting still I'd near perfected in the hospital. After the morgue and my relief that it wasn't Jeff, I felt I owed God. My prayer had been answered so the barter system kicked in. I couldn't swear off drink as I hadn't had one in months. So I went to the chemist, bought a pack of nicotine patches. This was my third day, and though I was in withdrawal, it wasn't as bad as I anticipated. The last remaining cigarettes in the packet, I put under the mattress. If the craving got unbearable, I'd have a crushed, crumpled solution. Listened to Warren Zevon – well, to one track. He knew he was dying and I was conscious of that, heard 'Knocking On Heaven's Door' as if I'd never heard the song before. It tore me apart and I knew I'd never be able to play it again.

Tried Emmylou. The title of the album, *Stumbling Into Grace*, seemed appropriate. No way I was going into grace other than like that. The second track, 'I Will Dream', had more than a touch of Irish influence, and not just the lyrics – a sadness of centuries. The fourth, 'Time In Babylon', seemed to be a statement on the current American psyche, but maybe I was just thinking too much. Then 'Strong Hand', a track for June Carter, came as close to saccharine as it gets, yet was uplifting in a melancholy style.

Perhaps it was the music, the isolation, the long empty hours, but try as I might, I couldn't blot out Serena May, Jeff's daughter. I'd loved her as much as I was ever going to be able to love anyone. I'd been minding her, but was unfocused, and she climbed out the window. Three years of age. My mind locked down, refused to play the chaos after.

I thought about Mrs Bailey, the times we talked. Never, not even once, had she lost faith in me. God knows, I've lost faith myself, climbing in and out of a bottle, receiving bad beatings, destroying everything I touched. Had never been able to get her to use my Christian name. I grieved for her.

With horror, I realized I cared for more people in the graveyard than in life, which means you've lived too long or God has a serious vendetta going, with no sign of Him letting up in the foreseeable future. What all this transmuted into was rage, a blinding, encompassing, white rawness of fury. When I hit the guy on the bridge, the truth was I felt near released. Only massive control prevented me finishing him off, and man, I wanted to – still did. The classic definition of depression is rage turned inward, so the way I figured it, I was born depressed. No fucking more. I wasn't going under that dank water which is depression, where your best daily moment is climbing into bed. Of course, the very worst is when you wake, the black cloud waiting, and you go 'Not this shit again.'

I was the cauldron waiting for the match. I bloody prayed for it. Deep down, I knew I was focusing on this stalker, glad he'd come along. The more I thought about him harassing Ridge, the more I simmered. I wanted to catch him, not for her but as a release for the tornado inside. Too, I fucking hate intimidation. Some asshole who crept around in the dark, preying unseen on a woman – oh man, I wanted him bad.

I was well aware I'd put Father Malachy on the back burner, tried to rationalize that I'd been en route to talk to one of Father Joyce's victims when the cops whisked me away to meet Clancy. Resolved to get right on it when Cody relieved me midweek.

Meanwhile, the time edged by and I was going nuts.

I wanted to lash out, to put my fist through the window. No sign of a stalker. I saw Ridge leave for work, then return at the end of her shift. What she looked was tired and even hungover – I know the signs.

Wednesday finally came and Cody appeared with a rucksack and a breezy attitude. I introduced him to the landlady and he charmed her completely. Produced an apple tart from Griffin's Bakery, so fresh that the aroma filled the house. The landlady was thrilled.

'Oh, I love apple tart.'

He took out a carton of cream and she was full won over. He said,

'You gotta have cream, am I right?'

She blushed, I swear she did, went,

'I shouldn't. I mean, a girl has to watch her figure.'

When I dragged him away, she was still cooing. He said to me, all business now,

'We're going to nail this guy, right?'

'I hope so.'

'Jack, come on, what's with the negative waves. Practise saying "I can and I will."'

He couldn't be bloody serious. I asked,

'Are you serious?'

'It's an affirmation, Jack. I say every morning, "Every day, in every way, I'm getting better—"'

I put up my hand, went,

'Jesus, enough, I get the picture.'

Knocked him back, but he was a trier, said,

'Works for me.'

He looked round the room, saw the CDs, asked,

'What's the sounds?'

'Emmylou Harris, Warren Zevon.'

'Who?'

I didn't have the patience or the inclination to tell him, so began to take my leave. He produced a small box, gift wrapped, handed it over. I asked,

'What's this?'

'A present to mark our bonding.'

Took the paper off and there was a mobile phone. He said,

'It's charged, with credit and ready to rock 'n' roll.'

I mumbled some lines of thanks and he said,

'No biggie.'

I looked at him, the eager beaver, full of ideals and spunk, asked,

'How far are you ready to go?'

'Go?'

'If we catch this guy, how far are you prepared to go, out on a limb?'

He was unsure, wanted to get it right, said,

'We'll, am, hand him over.'

My voice was scathing.

'To, like . . . the Guards – that your thinking?'

'Am, I guess.'

I shook my head and he asked, a hint of desperation now,

'What do you think, Jack? You're the pro.'

I wanted to fuck with him. Hell, I just wanted to fuck with anyone, said,

'Let me give you a clue, yeah?'

He waited. All the vim he'd garnered by buttering the landlady was leaking away and he nodded, anxiety plastered on his face. I said,

'I'll be getting a hurley, putting the steel rims on the end, ensuring it has that necessary *swoosh*. You catch my drift?'

He did, but didn't believe it, said,

'You mean, like a beating?'

I waited, then said,

'Think of it more as an affirmation.'

As I was leaving, the landlady stepped into the hall, cooed,

'What a lovely boy, is he your son?'

I denied him.

Walking towards town, I felt like I'd been released from prison. My limp wasn't bothering me, due in part to all the pacing I'd done the past few days. A guy, the worse for wear, fell in step beside me, asked,

'Remember me, Jack?'

I was all bummed out on civility, said,

'No.'

He stopped, let me examine him. About five eight, balding rapidly, watery eyes and a drinker's ruined face. Wearing a grey cardigan buttoned to the neck, shiny pants that gleamed from constant wear, slip-on grey shoes, a hole on the side of the left, he said,

'Minty . . . Minty Grey.'

Like a reject from Pop Idol, then I did remember – from schooldays, his nickname from the sweets he chewed on a regular basis. Two of his front teeth were black –

not just decayed, coal black. As if reading my mind, he said,

'I haven't had a mint in years.'

I said,

'Good to see you.'

Couldn't bring myself to use his nickname. The years bring, if not maturity, then a heightened sense of ridiculousness. He said,

'Did you hear about the Poor Clares?'

I hoped they hadn't been burned out or worse. These days, anything seemed possible. An enclosed order, they existed on donations. The terrible times of the fifties, they'd ring the bell when they were hungry, the sound of that tolling telling all that was horrible and shameful about poverty. Who could have forecast the Celtic Tiger? Gone were the days when priests went door to door, asking for dues, and people turned out the lights in the vain hope the priest would think no one was home. And I wondered why I had such rage. He said,

'They've gone online.'

Thought I misheard. Did he mean line dancing? Nuns drove cars, appeared on TV . . .

Then he added,

'They've got a website.'

'You're kidding – the Poor Clares?'

'Honest to God, it was on the news.'

I shook my head, asked,

'How do you . . . I mean . . . give alms?'

He gave a mega grin, black teeth prominent, said,

'They accept all the major credit cards.'

He stopped at the Bal, said,

'I'm going in here.'

I reached for some change and he said,

'No need, Jack, it's dole day. But thanks.'

He'd unnerved me, shook up the few illusions I'd kept. He laughed, said,

'If I'd a website, you could send me a few bob, use your credit card.'

I laughed unconvincingly, admitted,

'I don't have one.'

He gave me a thumbs up, said,

'But you've a good heart, best credit there is.'

Bank that.

On impulse, I headed for Shantalla to suss out Tom Reed, the guy who provided bouncers. I wondered if there was a vocation for that – you wake up one morning knowing with certainty your mission is to supply bouncers to the world. I found his house without any trouble, a two-storey with a well-tended garden. I took a deep breath, knocked at the door.

Showtime.

Always the moment I loved and loathed, never quite sure how I was going to broach the subject, the flat-out 'Are you a killer?'

A woman answered. She was in her twenties, looked harried, asked,

'Yes?'

'Is Tom around?'

She roared over her shoulder,

'Tom!'

And went back inside.

I could hear phones ringing – business was brisk. A short man, bald, with a barrel chest, jog pants and, I kid you not, a pink T-shirt with the logo WE BOUNCE appeared, went,

'Yeah?'

I put out my hand, said,

'I'm Jack Taylor. I wonder if I could have a few moments of your time?'

'You selling something?'

Go for broke. I said,

'It's about Father Joyce.'

A look of sheer agony crossed his face – raw, naked hurt, followed by a weariness. He sighed.

'This shit again.'

I tried to look sympathetic – not one of my strong suits, I come on like a chancer – said,

'I realize this must be difficult.'

He gave me a long look, asked,

'You a survivor?'

I knew he meant of child abuse, said,

'No.'

He put his head to the side, said,

'So you realize nothing.'

He considered, then,

'OK, I'll give you five minutes. The girl, she's my secretary, up to her arse in sales.'

I stepped in and pulled the door closed. He led the way to a kitchen, files and papers everywhere. I asked,

'Business good?'

'Yeah, a madhouse. I keep planning on renting office space, but Galway – who can afford it? Get you some coffee? We only got instant.'

'What I drink.'

While the kettle boiled, he asked,

'You a boozer?'

A statement more than a question. I tried for indignation and he said,

'It's in the eyes, that haunted look – I've been there. Other places too, none I'd like to revisit.'

He shovelled instant into mugs, added the water, said,

'We're out of milk, out of everything except demand for door personnel. That's bouncers to you and me.'

I was curious, asked,

'How'd you get into it?'

He motioned for me to sit. I did and he took a chair opposite, said,

'Much like you'd imagine. I was a bouncer, got tired of spit and worse in my face, figured I'd get into management. Seven years ago, when the town was seriously partying. If you were younger, I could have you working this evening.'

Not if Clancy got wind of it. I asked,

'How come?'

He drank off his coffee, said,

'You look thick.'

I let that lie, didn't want to explore what exactly he meant. I'd a fairly good idea it wasn't flattering. I said,

'I've been asked to look into Father Joyce's death.'

The fleeting pain again. He stood up, went to the sink, washed his mug with energy, said,

'So you come to the few people who'd the courage to speak out. Three of us who had the balls to talk, among the numerous others who were abused. Who's paying your freight? The Church? As they sure as hell ain't paying us. But they will. The Government's trying to shaft us too – I guess that's legal abuse. One sympathetic judge, Le Foy? They got her to resign.'

There was a ferocity in his words, a power that seemed to chill the air. In an attempt to diffuse it, I said,

'You've overcome . . . am . . . your past. I mean, you're functioning, doing well.'

He slammed a fist on the washboard, asked,

'How the fuck would you know? You see a wife here, kids, anything normal? I've been on every medication in the book, lost my hair when I was nineteen years old. You want to know what I do for recreation?'

He mouthed the word with every ounce of contempt he could summon, continued,

'I walk the frigging prom, up and down. I talk to no one, not a single human being. I watch TV. Comedies – *Seinfeld*, *Friends*, *South Park*, *Family Guy* – and you know what? I never laugh, not even once. And *Father Ted*, I'll never watch that, priests are never going to be funny. I died years ago, but my body won't lie down – isn't that a pisser? And family – forget it. I always thought I'd have a son, and like now, he could inherit the business. But thanks to that Father, the pervert, I'll die alone, no issue. A man should have a son, 'tis a real sin what was robbed from me.'

I was lost for a reply, so he asked,

'You want to know did I kill him . . . That's it, isn't it? You think a hundred other people don't want to ask me the very same thing? He buggered me ten times a week till I bled from me arse. I was nine years old when he started. When I told my mother, she leathered me till I couldn't walk.'

Sweat was pouring down his face, the pink T-shirt drenched. He continued,

'Sometimes, for variety, he'd stick it in my mouth. So am I sorry he's dead? I tell you what I am sorry about – that it was the head got cut off. They got the wrong end.'

I stood up, asked,

'Can I get you some water?'

He was spent, his whole body collapsed in on itself, shook his head, said,

'You'll want to see Michael?'

'Yes, I would.'

He gave a small twisted smile, said,

'You'll like Michael, he's got his shit together.'

I wanted to reach out, touch his shoulder and say, what? That it would be all right. Whatever else, it was never going to be that. I said,

'I appreciate your talking to me, the coffee . . .'

He seemed not to hear me. As I was heading out, he asked,

'You familiar with the term "cold case"?'

When I nodded, he said,

'That's what this is. Cold as granite.'

Then he added,

'You ever catch the guy who did it, do me a favour?'
'Yes?'
'Shake his hand for me.'

Later that evening, by one of those bizarre coincidences, *Sky News* reported a drive-by shooting in a small hamlet in Suffolk, alleged to be connected to a dispute between bouncers. Drive-by . . . how American we were getting.

Switched to the local news. The Guards stopped a speeding car. The occupants, teenagers in balaclavas, had in their possession

Two swords
Six Stanley knives
Baseball bats
Can of petrol.

Trick or treat.

13

'Diversion. Being unable to cure death,
wretchedness and ignorance,
men have decided, in order to be happy,
not to think about such things.'

Pascal, *Pensées*, 168

I'd my mobile phone and yes, Cody, it was switched on. Only two people had the number, Cody and Ridge.

So how busy was it going to be? Truth is, I kind of liked it. Small, silver, compact, seemed like a bullet casing. I was still wearing the patches but old compulsions go down reluctantly. I'd tap my pocket for the phone, think it was a pack of cigs. Cody suggested,

'Get a ring tone.'

Sounded like a visit to a hooker. I asked,

'Get what?'

'Your own personalized ring sound. I've Franz Ferdinand but you could get, like, Beyoncé or Black Eyed Peas.'

I didn't imagine Johnny Duhan was available, said,

'I'll settle for the sound of it ringing.'

For the life of me, I couldn't grasp the concept. There were companies who'd sell you a tune? Between that and supplying bouncers, where was the country going? Jesus.

I visualized being in church, no one's bothered to switch off the phones and a whole orchestra of pop tunes clashes in unison. Who knows, maybe they could replace the choir.

Cody determined to drag me up to speed, asked,
'You've web access, right?'
'Take a wild fucking guess.'
After I left Tom Reed, I walked down to the canal,
watched the ducks. And soon, of course, the darkness.
Closed my eyes, imagined Jeff's body drifting by. Every night
of the week, the Guards pulled someone from the water,
mostly too late. The range covered the city's population.
Into the water went

>Students
>Drunks
>The demented
>The lonely
>Young girls
>The sick
>The healthy.

So sang the song of the canals: give me your poor and
rejected.
No clergy.
Yet.
My phone rang, putting the heart crossways in me. I
answered, heard Cody, asked,
'What?'
'Just checking in, hoss.'
Hoss.
I asked,
'Any developments?'
'No Sir, but I'm on top of it, got my eyes peeled.'
He sounded like he was enjoying himself, and in amaze-
ment I asked,

'You're enjoying this?'

'Man, it's a blast.'

Every time I thought I'd a handle on him, got him part way sussed, he reached new levels of cliché. I said,

'Don't call me with hourly reports, got it?'

'Radio silence unless there's a code red?'

'Exactly.'

Was about to click off when he asked,

'What do you think about Mary?'

'Who?'

'The landlady's daughter. A fox, right?'

I clicked off.

He deserved her.

Truth to tell, I was jealous.

Saturday morning, I rang Cody. Took ages before he answered, then,

'Yeah . . .'

Sleep written all over it. I decided to crack the whip. I mean you're the boss, it's your moral duty. I snapped,

'You're sleeping?'

Before he could answer, I heard laughter, a girl's, and he said,

'Am, call you back . . .'

He didn't.

I was out, walking through the morning market. It was a bright day, the area thronged with people, few of them Irish, let alone Galwegians. A couple from Denmark were selling sausages roasting on an open grill – the aroma blanketed the crowd. I might have been tempted but a line of people were waiting. Instead, I looked at some stained-glass reproductions of the Claddagh.

And the seller said,

'Give you a good price, Guv.'

Guv!

Jesus, Camden Lock in the west of Ireland. I was intrigued, asked,

'You a Londoner?'

'A Geordie.'

'Oh right.'

And for the life of me, I couldn't think of another word, another word that didn't involve shepherd's pie or some such supposedly Geordie cliché. He said,

'I've been here five years.'

Got me vocal again, and with huge originality I asked,

'Like it?'

He gave me a look of confusion, asked,

'What's not to like? The pubs, the crack.'

I felt I should say something but my phone went and he said,

'Saved by the bell.'

I answered, ready to light a fire under Cody, heard,

'Jack?'

'Ridge . . .'

She was crying, or as close to that as she'd ever come, said,

'My car, it's contaminated.'

Instead of asking what the hell that meant, I asked,

'Where are you?'

'The cathedral car park.'

'Stay there, I'm five minutes away.'

As I fought my way out of the market, I noticed a guy selling T-shirts that read,

> Every dog has its day.
> Don't plan on it being
> anytime soon.

Amen to that.

As I hurried along Market Street, I noticed a headline on a newspaper:

Reich or wrong.

Arnold had become Governor of California. The bottom part of the page related how the English team were threatening to strike, and if they refused to travel to Turkey, they were out of Euro 2004. Ireland had their crunch match due against Switzerland in a few days. I digested all that, thought, 'I'm returning to life,' bizarre as it was. I crossed the Salmon Weir Bridge just as an angler was landing a fine fish. It pained me to see such a beautiful specimen have its head smashed against a rock. The sound like an omen.

Ridge was sitting on the low wall circling the car park. Mass was letting out and I saw people dip their fingers in the Holy Water font, bless themselves, '*In anim an Athair* . . . In the Name of the Father.'

The English translation just didn't work, not for me, not in my heart where it mattered.

Ridge was smoking a cigarette.

I couldn't have been more surprised if she'd been toting a sawn-off or snorting coke. I thought, is she going to pick up my addictions, one by one? She was wearing a white sweatshirt, faded jeans and scuffed Reeboks. Her face was haggard. I asked,

'You OK?'

How lame was that?

And got the prerequisite lash.

'How the hell do you think I am?'

She pointed a finger, said,

'It's there.'

She didn't look at the car, added,

'The doors are open, the . . . item . . . is in the back seat.'

I approached cautiously, my nerves shot to ribbons. There was a note pinned to the steering wheel.

> You hore of Babylon
> Yer time is near.

A clue. He couldn't spell.

The church bells began to ring. Jeez, talk about timing.

Ask not . . .

I didn't.

What was beating in my mind, uncalled and certainly unwanted, was Warren Zevon, 'Knocking On Heaven's Door'.

Especially the bit asking to take the badge offa me.

Oh yeah.

In the back seat was a pair of knickers. I got my pen,

used it to move them and could see the still-damp semen.
The mind locks on a detail, some minute item to block the
evidence. The knickers had tiny hearts embroidered on the
front and that ripped through my guts like fucking acid.
There was a Supermac's bag littering the floor. I got it and
deposited the knickers in it, put the bag in my pocket. My
phone rang. I answered with a terse,

'Yeah?'

'Jack, it's Cody. I've got great news.'

Could we get so lucky? I said,

'Tell.'

He sounded breathless, said,

'Mary and I are an item.'

I actually held the phone away from me, as if it was
pulling a fast one, then I gritted,

'You're fucking having me on?'

He read me wrong, thought I was pleased, gushed,

'Isn't it unbelievable? She's such a catch.'

Ridge was staring at the pocket where I'd pushed the
crumpled bag, then, as if in defiance, lit another cig, blew
the smoke at me. I said to Cody,

'I'll tell you what's unbelievable. While you're romancing
your . . .'

Words failed me momentarily. Then I focused, white heat
in my brain, said,

'Fox. While you're at that, the stalker has defiled our
lady's car.'

I could hear his intake of breath, then,

'Defiled . . . what . . . I . . . ?'

'You're fucking fired is what you are.'

And I hit the Off button.

Ridge gave what in other circumstances might have passed for a smile, asked,

'You fired somebody – did I miss a chapter? When did you begin hiring people, never mind firing?'

I waved that away, asked,

'How long was your car there?'

She stubbed the cigarette on the wall, short stabbing movements that reflected her state of mind, said,

'I went to Mass.'

Paused.

Expecting what? Derision, surprise? I said nothing, had been a Mass attendee for a time there myself. She continued,

'And when I came out, I found . . . the message . . . and in case you didn't detect it, he broke the side window.'

Yeah, I missed that.

She stared at my pocket, asked,

'You're keeping the evidence for like . . . what, a DNA test?'

I wanted to slap her, slap somebody, said,

'I need you to do something.'

She waited, tapping her fingers on the wall. I wanted to say,

'Like first, have some fucking manners.'

Went with,

'Think hard about anyone you've arrested over the past few years. I'm thinking especially of anyone who threatened you, who would come back at you.'

She stood up, said,

'Like that's going to help. What, do you think every

thug I arrested treated me decently? God, you were a
Guard – they all threaten you, or is it so long ago you can't
remember?'

She began to walk away and I asked,

'What about your car?'

Without breaking stride, she said,

'Fuck my car.'

An elderly churchgoer, passing, looked at me, said,

'Young ladies today, the language of them.'

I said,

'Trust me, that's no lady.'

14

'The eternal silence of those infinite spaces fills me with dread.'

Pascal, *Pensées*, 206

1957. Galway, the week before Easter.

With the ten shillings the priest had given him, the boy bought a mountain of chocolate. Sitting on the toilet, the wrappers strewn at his feet, the boy felt his stomach heave, then vomit poured from his mouth. The boy almost welcomed this, it distracted him from the bleeding in his rectum. He reached for another bar, nausea rising, and shoved a chunk into his mouth. It sometimes stopped him thinking about Sunday, serving mass and what happened after. Six weeks ago his mother had asked him what he was giving up for Lent and he said chocolate, and began to giggle uncontrollably.

He reached for another bar.

I've read tons of crime fiction. I'm especially fond of the private-eye stuff. All alcoholics are doomed romantics and the notion of the lone outsider pitting against the odds, it's like the line from the movie, 'You gotta love him.'

All those books are fond of the term *dogged*. Bearing

that in mind, I stayed with the priest case. Time to see the second suspect, the engineer, Michael Clare. Doggedly, I checked the phone directory, got his business listing, rang and was greeted by a secretary. A very cheerful one, so cheerful that I suspected sarcasm. Like this:

'Michael Clare's office, may I be of assistance?'

Her voice had an upbeat that suggested nothing would make her happier than to be of such. She had to be kidding. In Ireland, the only English-ism we've adopted with eagerness is surliness. Usually, you phone a company, you get,

'What?'

Like you interrupted them during foreplay.

So I was a little thrown, mumbled I was a friend of bouncer supplier Tom Reed and he'd suggested Mr Clare might be able to *assist* me. She asked,

'Would you mind holding for a tiny moment and I'll check his timetable?'

Mind?

Then,

'Mr Clare is free at noon. Might I take your name, please?'

'Jack Taylor.'

'Is noon convenient for you, Mr Taylor?'

I vouchsafed it was, and she finished with,

'We shall expect you then.'

She didn't add *Have a good day* but it was implied.

How American are we?

I'd a while to wait so I tried again to listen to music. Slapped on the earphones, got Johnny Cash going. His granite voice was as old as the stones in Connemara. Then the Nine Inch Nails song, 'Hurt'.

Oh fuck.

Murderous lyrics, the truth of them lashing every part of my being. Recovering alcoholics have a hard on for the Kristofferson song, 'One Day At A Time'. Dirge on. Every time you hear it, you go,

'Sweet Jesus.'

And not from reverence.

They ought to make 'Hurt' mandatory at the door of AA meetings, ask,

'Does this song have relevance to you, does it lacerate you?'

If not, fuck off.

It opened such corridors of pain – the deaths of Sean, the Grogans' proprietor; Brendan Cross, ex-Guard; the tinkers, six of them; my parents; Warren Zevon; and, oh God, Serena May.

And a lot more. So when Johnny started sneering about an empire of dirt, I had to rip the headphones off. My hands were shaking. I blamed the nicotine patches. Here I was, patched, sober and bewildered. Had been to the Age Concern shop again, spent thirty euros – a fortune in a charity shop – and donned the fruits of my trip. Black jacket of a suit, white T-shirt, black jeans, Timberland boots.

Checked my reflection.

Mix and match.

If you liked the Undertaker-shops-at-Gap image, it was fine. Still, it was in the vague neighbourhood of *respectable*, and yet hinted I was cool, clued in. The lies we tell ourselves, every fucking day. The alternative is to stay in bed, a loaded pistol under your pillow. In a flurry of extravagance, I'd bought some Polo aftershave. Well, the assistant was pretty and I'm an idiot, fool for love, how are you? They were all out of Brut, else who knows? Splashed the stuff on and it stung like the bad word. I was ready to investigate, smelling if not like a rose then certainly like someone who had little contact with reality.

For no discernible reason, a line sprang to me mind . . . *The child is father to the man.*

What the fuck was with that?

And more importantly, who said it? Tennyson, Browning, one of the Brit heavyweights, anyway.

Michael Clare's office was in the Dun Aengus building. Situated at the end of Long Walk, you couldn't find a more prestigious address, right along from my solicitor. You hear that – out of the home for the bewildered and mouthing, *my solicitor*. What the building said was . . . money, money, money.

Lots of.

Long Walk is among my favourite routes. You pass under the Spanish Arch then along by the water, the Claddagh right across. Nimmo's Pier marks the point. Before you lies Galway Bay, you can almost see the Aran Islands. I ever get lucky or seriously rich, that's where I'm headed, as a base if nothing else. The sound of the seagulls, the smell of the ocean, you gulp deep breaths and want to mouth a rosary of gratitude. It should be mandatory for artists to live here, an oasis of the soul. And if it's a bright day, Sweet Jesus, you are elected.

It was a very bright day.

The building was all glass and light, seemed to shimmer like a mirage.

The receptionist, young, pretty, breezed,

'Good morning.'

'It certainly is. I'm Jack Taylor, to see Mr Clare.'

She seemed happy with my mission, said,

'Have a seat, Sir, I'll buzz him. Would you like some tea, coffee?'

'Am, no, I'm good.'

Five minutes later, I was shown into Clare's office. The décor was Zen inspired, no frills, Spartan in its appearance. There was one of John Behan's sculptures in his office, a bronze bull. I was very taken with it. Wanted to say *my solicitor* has a similar piece.

I don't usually know if a man is good looking – guys aren't good on that type of information.

I did now.

He was gorgeous and knew it. The spit of Michael Landon, who starred in *Little House on the Prairie*. He was also in that sickening series about an angel, a Waltons with wings. Michael Clare was tall, tanned, and dressed in a seriously expensive suit. He must have been fifty, but could have passed for late thirties.

The fucker.

He extended his hand, said,

'You like the Behan bull? Give me a word to describe it.'

'Am, brave?'

He liked it, smiled, his hand still extended, asked,

'Mr Taylor, can my girl get you anything?'

I took his hand and he near crushed my fingers. It's a macho thing, vying for supremacy. I said,

'No thank you, she offered already, and please, call me Jack.'

He was delighted or looked it, released my bruised hand, moved behind a massive desk, sat, smiled, looked at the bull again, said,

'Brave, interesting description for that piece of work, but you're not here to discuss art . . . So it's Jack, well, in that case I'm Michael. What can I do for you?'

Why was he being so gracious? He had to know I was looking into the murder of the priest, that by implication he was suspect. His accent was not outright British but definitely pointed in that direction. What the Irish grudgingly term *polished*. I said,

'I spoke to Tom Reed about the death of Father Joyce.'

He was shaking his head, resignation in his face, said,

'Poor Tom, a sad man.'

'Yeah, why's that?'

He smiled – glorious teeth, white, capped, shining. I'd great teeth too, but they weren't my own. He said,

'Come on, Jack, the man's a basket case.'

I was surprised, showed it, said,

'He seemed to have it reasonably together.'

He gave me a tolerant smile – one of my favourite expressions, gets me cranked – said,

'How easily duped you are.'

Duped, me?

Before I could answer, my phone shrilled. I made that face you do when you feel a horse's ass, muttered,

'Should have turned it off.'

He shrugged, said,

'Answer it and I'll organize some coffee.'

He left the office as I said,

'Yes?'

'Jack, it's Cody. Don't hang up.'

'What do you want?'

I had granite in there. He caught it, blurted,

'I found him.'

Excited, jubilant, high, I asked,

'Found who?'

'The stalker. I got him.'

I was amazed, but would I let up?

Nope.

Went,

'So, what, I've got to beg for the details?'

His joy cooled. He said,

'Sorry, I . . . am . . . His name is Sam White, he lives in St Patrick's Avenue . . .'

He paused, waited. I snapped,

'Age, occupation?'

'Oh right, he's twenty-eight, unemployed . . . and lives alone.'

'You sure it's him?'

'Positive.'

'OK, I'll meet you in Richardson's pub at seven this evening. Think you can find it?'

I could hear his hurt. He said,

'Yes, yes, I can.'

I clicked the Off.

Hard ass to the end.

* * *

162

Michael Clare returned with two steaming mugs, handed one over, said,

'Didn't figure you for the cup-and-saucer type.'

Could take that any number of ways. Alcoholics dread saucers, spoons, anything that lets the shakes show. See the spoon do a jig as the saucer does a full fandango. Or is it that he had me pegged as rough, unaccustomed to the niceties? Or, fuck, maybe it was simply convenient.

He smiled, as if he'd read my mind, asked,

'Milk, cream, sugar?'

'Black's good.'

It was.

I tried to get back on track, asked,

'You were saying Tom wasn't too . . . together?'

He sat fixing the crease in his pants, said,

'You don't let up, do you? What do you say, we get to it? I'm a busy man and you . . .' He indicated my phone, '. . . have a life. Let's stop dancing around. Just ask me.'

So I asked,

'Did you have anything to do with the . . . the . . . demise . . . of . . . Father Joyce?'

He seemed to taste *demise*, roll it round in his head. Such a question should have sparked

Outrage

Indignation.

At the very least, the bum's rush.

But he leaned back in his chair, used his hands to massage the back of his neck, stared at the ceiling. Something had entered the room. I'm not fanciful enough to term it a chill, but it was definitely a drop in temperature. He asked,

'You ever do yoga, Jack?'

The use of my first name seemed like an obscenity, and his friendly, near jokey tone was spooky, caught me blind-side. I fumbled, then,

'No, I don't have the patience.'

Then he snapped back into an upright position, one fluid movement, said,

'You should. You're very tense – wound up, one might say.'

Is there an answer to this? Because I didn't have one. He looked at me, said,

'The answer to your question is, yes.'

Case solved.

Would it were so easy. Yeah, like that is ever going to happen. You've been a Guard, it's a rule of thumb, a person confesses right off the bat, it stinks to high heaven. After a high-profile murder, the cops are inundated with confessions. And I knew instinctively, Clare enjoyed fucking my head. I could see it in his face. Also, someone confesses so easily, it is often a cover for the real perpetrator. A mother will confess to save her son, or a father.

Translate: easy confession equals horseshite.

Fold my tent, call the Guards.

He stood up, all brisk efficiency, asked,

'Anything else?'

I stood, perplexed and lost, tried,

'You admit it?'

He put a finger to his lips, made the sound,

'Sh . . . sh.'

Then he levelled his gaze on me, as if he were studying a specimen, and not a very interesting one, said,

'Realpolitik.'

And pronounced it in a German guttural tone. When I stared at him blankly, he asked,

'Perhaps you're more familiar with our American friends' use of the term *juice*. Let me give you a very brief picture of how things work, me boy.'

The condescension in *me boy* threw me into a boiling anger, building a notch at a time. He continued,

'Power – the fuel that really runs things, how stuff gets taken care of. I play golf with your old buddy Superintendent Clancy, a man who is not fond of you, I'm afraid. Think of golf as our version of the Masons, those who golf together save their arse together. Now stretch your mind, can you do that? Can you think outside your little box? Imagine an unholy trinity – the Church, the Guards, and me fein (myself) – we want to see this town grow, we have major plans, and you think a small disruption like a dead priest, who is a disgrace to the Church anyway, is going to – how shall I put it – rock the boat?'

He emitted a short laugh, more like a bark, a rabid one, then,

'In situations of major development – and make no mistake, Taylor, this town is going to be the cultural capital of Europe – if I may be excused a tiny pun, heads are going to roll.'

He paused, in love with the flow of his rhetoric, the images of major importance coming down the pike, and then he injected granite into his voice, asked,

'You think a half-arsed investigator, a sodden dick, a private fecking eye, for heaven's sake, a shamus – Good God Almighty, you think a nothing like you is going to impede the flow? And you've already had one warning, if I'm not mistaken.'

The so-called mugging outside the Furbo Suite and the Guards shoes, it was all making sinister sense.

I was as enraged as I've ever been. Not even by the insults – and they were noted, by Jesus they were – but that he really thought he could just roll over anything and everybody. That truly had me spitting iron. You spit iron, you are one beat from coronary aggravation. I muttered,

'You bastard, you think I'm so easy to intimidate?'

And yeah, I know, lame.

His phone shrilled, least that's how it sounded to me, and he said,

'You're dismissed. Be a good boy and bury yourself in a bottle, it's what you do best.'

As he picked up the receiver, he reached in his jacket, pulled out his wallet and took a twenty, threw it across the desk, said,

'Here, I'll get you started.'

I was that close to making him eat it.

I stood shakily, as if I'd just thrown back a large Jameson, and walked out of there so riled my eyes were actually emitting water.

I got outside and had to draw heavy deep breaths to try and bring my anger down. I think ten minutes may have passed before I got some semblance of sanity, then for some reason I looked back at the building.

He stood inside the glass window, another Behan work, 'Ellis Island', behind him, and stared out, his eyes as lifeless as the glass dividing us. Then he turned on his heel and was gone.

15

'All men naturally hate each other.'

Pascal, *Pensées*, 451

I went to Eyre Square with the slim hope of maybe finding Jeff. Perhaps he'd rejoined the drinking school. The sun was in that Irish mode, playing with us, one minute in full sight and you took off your jacket, thinking,

'Ah, thank Christ.'

Then as soon as it saw commitment from you, it vanished and you were frozen in a force-five wind that sprang from sheer badness. A tinker had said to me once,

''Tis not that people kill themselves in Ireland, Jack, that's no mystery, with the fierce weather. The mystery is that more don't.'

Argue that.

Renovations were in full swing. The trees were gone, like civility, and workmen were already digging up the park, driving jackhammers into the green fresh soil. There's some deep metaphor there but it's too sad to draw. I managed to grab one of the few remaining benches and watched the drinking school, huddled in what looked like a scrum. If Jeff was among them, I couldn't see him. A woman approached and something in the tilt of her head was familiar. She was average height with mousy brown hair, a hesitancy in her walk, like a person who has been mugged and has never recovered. Her face – oh God, I knew that face.

Cathy.

What a history we had. She'd been a punk rocker who washed up in Galway with a hell of a singing voice and an even more hellish heroin habit. She'd kicked the drug, I had her help me on a case and then introduced her to Jeff.

They'd married, had Serena May, and I'd fucked that to all damnation.

I hadn't seen her since the child was buried, and thankfully, couldn't remember what, if anything, she'd said to me.

My impulse was to run and as fast as I could, but my legs went weak. She stood before me, boring into my eyes. Whatever light blazed there – and something dark was definitely burning – it wasn't forgiveness. She said,

'Jack Taylor.'

She was in her early thirties, I reckon, but she looked a bad fifty, deep lines under her eyes and around her mouth. Whoever said grief ennobles has never lost a child. I stood up and she sneered,

'Manners? Or are you running?'

If only I could.

I tried,

'Cathy . . .'

And not another word would come to me. All the books I'd read, not worth a toss. My beloved Merton was sure to have a piece on this awesome sorrow but he wasn't providing it that day.

She squared up to me, there is no other term for it, right in my face.

'How have you been, Jack? Getting the drinks in, are you?'

No point in saying I wasn't drinking, no point in any words, but finally I managed,

'I am so sorry, you have no idea, I . . .'

I wanted to tell her that I'd been locked up in the asylum for months, that I carried the cross of her child every living moment, that I couldn't bear to look at any children without my very soul being seared.

I didn't.

I may have sighed. I certainly wanted to, I wanted to weep till the rivers ran dry.

Her body language was, to put it mildly, combative, and she was dressed for the event. Black leather waistcoat, black track bottoms, black trainers and black to blackest expression. She asked,

'Cat got your tongue? No pithy quote for me, none of your philosophical meanderings from all those oh so important books, like the one you were reading when you were supposed to be minding my little girl?'

Christ.

Her accent.

When I first met her, she'd a London one, all hard edges, attitude leaking from every syllable and I liked it, it was different, it was, well . . . it was her. She was one of the few genuine outlaws I'd met. The pose was real, if that's not too much of an Irish contradiction. She'd recently kicked heroin and was a bundle of raw exposed nerves. And that singing voice, like a dark bewitched angel, not so much fallen from grace as plunged.

Then she married Jeff and went native. Became more Irish than us. Didn't quite take to wearing shawls but was pretty close. Adopted a brogue that was unsettling in the extreme, a hybrid thing that was neither UK or Eire but some bastardized stage Irish gig.

That was gone.

Her London edge was back with a vengeance, rough cadence with a spread of bitterness that kicked you in the teeth.

In my despair, I asked just about the worst thing. Even now, I marvel at the depth of my crassness. I asked,

'How have you been?'

I cringe at the words.

She emitted a harsh laugh, fuelled with rage and savagery. Echoed me.

'How have I been?'

Let it hang there, let me savour the sheer awfulness of the query. Then,

'Well, lemme see, since I buried my daughter and lost my husband, I've been . . . fucking hunky dory. Went back to London, the shithole, went back to heroin, the beauty, and was dying as fast as I could manage it, but hey, guess what?'

She waited, like I had a notion, a single idea of what she could possibly mean, then she added,

'I had that light-bulb moment, you know the one Oprah talks about. I could see you in Galway, tossing back the pints, reading your books, and it galvanized me. I got clean and got me a mission – to find my husband. Or rather, to get you to find my husband. And here's a kicker – I learned how to shoot. Took my mind off shooting up. You find things, right, Jack? It's what you do. So find my husband. I, meanwhile, will be trying to find a rifle. I do have a slight problem – I can't seem to get my aim up. When I want a head shot, it keeps hitting low. You know about that Jack, don't you? Hitting low.'

The tone of her voice was ice, dripping with a coldness that would raise goosebumps on a corpse. Of all the freaking things, I was thinking of Elvis Costello, *My Aim Is True*.

Now she added,

'And you know what? You don't find him, alive of course, I'm going to kill you. As you Irish are fond of saying, *'Tis a pity*. Well, it's a real pity you don't have a child, Jack. We could even the score real easy. You took my daughter, so . . .'

Let that awful threat hang a moment in all its stark evil, then in a very chatty tone, very matter of fact, added,

'You always had a flair for drama. Well, dramatize this. Look up at the skyline, see the rooftops – I'll be on one, and aiming at what passes for your stone miserable fucking heart. I should have corrected my tendency to go low by then. You have a good day now, ta ra.'

The note of cheerfulness she injected into that *ta ra* may be the most chilling thing I've ever heard.

16

*'The echoes drawn
the pain through years.'*

Bewitched, KB

Christina Aguilera, as a nun, at an awards ceremony, strips off, wowing the audience.

Christ.

The afternoon, I went to a man named Curtin, in his seventies, part of a dying breed. He made hurleys. Located in Prospect Hill, he had a small shop with no sign – he didn't need to advertise. I greeted him and he took a moment to adjust his vision, asked,

'Young Taylor?'

God bless him.

He honed the hurleys from the ash, took weeks to get one exactly right. I gave him the specifications, the vital element being what the Irish call the *give*, the way the stick bends, what gives it that swoosh. You have to be able to hear it, else forget it. He listened, then,

'I'll have it in a month.'

I hated to fuck with an artist, but . . .

'I need one now.'

He was appalled, snapped,

'Go to a sports shop.'

Finally, he gave me what he considered inferior stock. Got him to further compromise his craft by putting iron bands on the end. When I paid him, he gave me a look of true disappointment, said,

'Young Taylor, you could have been a fine hurler.'

Only fine? I went,

'Not great?'

He turned away, said,

'There's very few Kerrs.'

Arguably the greatest player of our time.

Before meeting Cody, I rang Father Malachy, said,

'The case is closed.'

'What? You're giving up?'

I grimaced, said,

'I found the killer.'

I'd called him on my mobile. I was standing outside Griffin's Bakery, the smell of fresh bread enticing though I had no appetite. The Black Eyed Peas were playing in a nearby clothes shop. Hell, they were everywhere, had been Number One in the charts for ages. The song, 'Where Is The Love?'

Like I'd ever know.

Only much later did I learn the song was about 9/11. The band had been together since 1998, proving endurance sometimes pays dividends. A lesson I needed to apply. Father Malachy asked,

'Who is he?'

'Meet me, I'll tell you then.'

We fixed noon the next day. He ended with,

'I can't believe you found the fucker.'

From a priest!

He pronounced it in the Roscommon fashion . . . *Fooker*. Gives the word an added dimension and leaves you in no doubt as to the intent.

People round me were discussing the latest outrage in Limerick. That town had exploded in tribal/gang warfare. A man barely out of his teens, accused of murder, had been sensationally released. Due to 'witness intimidation', according to popular belief, the case against him had collapsed. The youth, emerging from the courthouse, gave the two-fingered salute to the media.

Almost of equal interest was Ireland losing to Australia in the quarter finals in rugby. Keith Woods, the captain, in tears, announcing his retirement.

Tough days.

And they were about to get a whole lot tougher.

Back at my apartment, I showered, had a double-spooned coffee, dressed for a beating. I put the hurley in a holdall, wore a black T-shirt that bore the faded logo

Knicks kiss ass.

Not exactly appropriate to Galway, but what had logic to do with this deal? Black cords, black boots. For nostalgia, for reassurance, item 8234, the Garda coat. A woman had thrown it on a fire and it still carried a hint of flame. Now that seemed appropriate.

Evening was coming in. I checked myself in the mirror, saw a grim face, rage in the eyes, the way I wanted it.

Cody was nervous when we hooked up. He was wearing a tracksuit, trainers and a suede jacket. His eyes were wary. He said,

'Good to see you, Jack.'

'Yeah, whatever.'

I looked at him, asked,

'How did you find him?'

He was excited, delighted at his ingenuity, said,

'Mary, the landlady's daughter, and I . . .'

He actually seemed embarrassed, but continued,

'We were, you know, fooling around in her bedroom, and out of the corner of my eye I saw this guy, hanging around outside your friend's house.'

I was amazed. At his age, if I was *fooling around* with a girl, I wouldn't have seen a damn thing out of my eye, I'd have had eyes for her, nothing else. He continued,

'I stood up and Mary wasn't pleased, I had to shush her. Mad, isn't it? As if the guy could have heard me.'

He looked at me for some praise, but I said nothing so he went on,

'I watched him cruise her house twice, and something in the tilt of his head, I knew this wasn't a casual stroll. Then he looked around in a furtive way and I knew, knew it was him, and I actually shouted that. Mary was asking . . . *Who?*'

He had to pause for a breath, he was reliving the chase, said,

'I pulled me jeans on and told her I had to go. She was annoyed but I said I'd make it up to her. I tracked him for two days, followed him into pubs, betting shops, and of course three times to your friend's house. He even tried the door and I got to see his face, his expression. I swear, Jack, it was full of . . . hate and . . . lust. I knew it was him.'

The classic procedure of tailing he'd picked up from cop shows. Did I tell him he'd done well?

No.

He glanced at the holdall and I said,

'It's a persuader.'

Waited for him to ask what that meant, but he went with,

'This Sam White, he's stalked women before, was even in court, but the woman withdrew the charges.'

I nodded and he asked,

'Are we going to report him?'

I nearly laughed, said,

'We had this conversation before, remember? I asked you if you were up to doing what had to be done.'

He was fading by the minute. Whatever resolve had gotten him this far was leaking fast. He tried,

'But maybe the Guards . . . ?'

'Maybe bollocks.'

More fiercely than I intended and I could see I scared him. I eased, not much but a little, said,

'The Guards might, I emphasize *might*, caution him. Then guess what? He'll up the ante, he'll do real damage.'

He went for broke.

'What are you going to do with . . . to . . . him?'

I began walking, said,

'Caution him, but with conviction.'

St Patrick's Avenue used to consist of a small lane connecting the church to Eyre Square, compact homes that housed a batch of true Galwegians. Like everything else, those people are scattered and gone. I could have named the members of each household. Who'd want to hear them?

Now they're townhouses.

Jesus.

You're sitting in a flash hotel, some asshole in a flashier suit is telling a babe,

'For weekends, I've a little pad in St Patrick's Avenue.'

I want to jump up, grab him by his Armani tie, roar,

'You know what happened to the people who lived there?'

And if I beat him from then till Christmas, he'd never know what I was on about. Or care.

Sam White's house was midway up the avenue, a light in the front window. I said,

'He's home.'

Cody looked like he might bolt. I asked,

'You want to take off?'

The idea heavily appealed but he tugged at his hair, went,

'No, it's, am . . . we'll be restrained, won't we?'

Lovely word. I tasted it, let it roll between my teeth, then,

'When he jerked off into her knickers, threw them on the back seat of her car while she was at church, at Mass, for Chrissakes . . .'

I had to take a deep breath, then,

'You think he showed restraint there, eh? That what you'd call it, is it?'

He shook his head, the picture of misery.

I knocked on the door, heard a TV being turned down. The door opened. He was in his late twenties, aiming at thirty. Tall, with a shaved head, wearing a singlet and tracksuit bottoms, bare feet, his toenails needed clipping. He was built like an athlete, worked out. Even features marred by a bad nose, light-blue eyes with a faint blood-shot tint. He asked,

'Help you?'

Dublin accent, not the north side but the more affluent belt, south of the Liffey – Dublin four, I'd guess. I said,

'May we see your TV licence?'

He was instantly angry, said,

'I'm unemployed.'

I gave Cody a long-suffering look, like we'd heard this a hundred times, asked,

'Did I ask you about your working status?'

'No . . . but . . .'

'So let's see some documentation – your social-security book. Maybe you're entitled to a free licence.'

Gave him my affable expression. Us blue-collar guys, in this together. Suggested I might be about to cut him some slack. His anger eased, if not a lot. He was a guy who liked to keep it simmering, figured his temper helped him blast his way through most situations. He asked,

'Couldn't it wait till, like, another time? *Top of The Pops* is on.'

I glanced at Cody, then, my voice full of enthusiasm,

'Hey, I want to see that. What do you think, Missy Elliott get to Number One? That Riverdance piece she uses, got black kids learning Irish dance, how cool is that?'

He was thrown. To him I was old, but hip? Before he could do the maths, I stepped inside, said,

'You get the papers, we'll keep an eye on the telly.'

He was moving down the hall, not sure how he'd been outdanced but going with it. Cody closed the door, looked at me, mouthed, *Missy Elliott?* I turned into the living room. Single guy's pad, a recliner seat like Chandler and Joey have on *Friends*, a can of Bud on the arm, tabloids scattered on the table, the Dublin Gaelic football team framed on the wall. Bookshelves crammed with videos, CDs and car magazines but no books.

The TV was one of those widescreen jobs, cost an arm and a leg. I unzipped the bag, Cody behind me, fretting, took out the hurley, got a firm grip. I was mid swing, the swoosh beginning its song, as Sam came into the room. It hit the screen with a massive bang, shattering it. Sam's jaw dropped. I said,

'We'll have to wait till next week to see what's Number One.'

Then pivoted and with a second swing took his feet from under him. Cody had his hand up. I ignored him. Sam on the floor, moaning, managed,

'For a TV licence?'

I nearly laughed. Instead, I swung my boot, broke his nose, let him feel that. Then I pulled him up, shoved him into the recliner. Blood was pouring into his mouth. I snapped at Cody,

'Get a cloth, for fuck's sake.'

He headed for the kitchen. I hunkered down, said,

'You can tell I'm a fairly intense guy, so when I ask you a question, bear that in mind.'

I reached in the holdall, got out the can, doused him with

petrol, then took a disposable lighter. His eyes went huge.
I said,

'You lie to me once, you're toast, got it?'

He nodded. I asked,

'Why are you terrorizing Guard Ridge?'

I gave the lighter an experimental flick and a bright flame
leaped out. His body shaking, he said,

'She arrested me for pissing on the street. In court, it
sounded like I'd exposed myself. Got a five-hundred-euro
fine and the label "sex offender".'

I stared at him, said,

'You go near her again, I'll kill you . . . believe me?'

He nodded. I slapped him open-handed on the face, twice,
hard, said,

'Let me hear you.'

'I swear, Jesus, I'll never go near her.'

I stood, put the hurley and can in the holdall, tapped his
bald head, said,

'Get a TV licence.'

As I turned I near collided with Cody, who had a wad
of tissues in his hand. I said,

'He won't be needing them, we're done.'

Cody glanced towards the figure slumped in the recliner,
then followed me out.

I closed the front door quietly and walked quickly down
the lane, my limp not bothering me at all. Cody, catching
up, asked,

'Did you kill him?'

17

*'There is no doctrine better suited to man
than that which teaches him his dual capacity
for receiving and losing grace.'*

Pascal, *Pensées*, 524

AA members would understand my behaviour, I'd be no mystery at all. No drink and no programme. I was doing what they call *white-knuckled sobriety*. Further, a dry drunk.

How did I remember this shit?

How could I not?

Near my new home, on the corner where Eyre Square hits Merchant's Road, is a new off-licence. I'd told Cody to go home, we'd speak soon. I walked straight into the bottle shop. A non-national was arguing with the assistant, claiming that he'd given a fifty-euro note, not a ten. I stared at the top shelf, the labels singing to me. The argument at the counter seemed in no danger of ending, so I said to the non-national,

'You want to move it along, pal?'

He spun round, prepared for fight, got a look at my face, opted for flight.

The assistant watched him go, muttered,

'Fucker.'

Then to me,

'Thanks for helping out.'

He was young, twenty maybe, and already steeped in bitterness. I nodded, said,

'Give me a bottle of Early Times, a dozen cans of Guinness.'

He had to reach for the bourbon, got it down, stared at the label, said,

'I never tasted that.'

Was he going to start now?

When I didn't reply, he went,

'Right, and a dozen Guinness?'

Got them packed in a plastic bag and said,

'You get a free T-shirt, any purchases over forty euro – you're entitled.'

Seeing I wasn't delirious at my luck, he jammed the shirt into the bag, said,

'I guess large.'

I paid him, asked,

'This your full-time job?'

'Jaysus no, I'm doing Accountancy.'

I took the bag, said,

'You've all the qualities.'

I was outside when I heard him add,

'I didn't charge you for the plastic bag.'

In the two years since the levy was imposed on them, the litter problem in the country had been halved. I muttered,

'Way to go.'

A guy leaning against a doorway asked,

'Help another human being?'

I gave him the T-shirt.

Then Jeff's face loomed large and I turned back, said to the guy,

'God just smiled on you.'

Handed him the whole batch of booze . . . I was half a street away when I heard him shout,

'More like the devil.'

Argue with that?

I didn't.

I had been pacing the floor of my apartment. I was still on high dough. The adrenalin surge hadn't abated and the ever-present rage wasn't sated. I shucked off my coat, put a CD on.

Arranged the props and the lights.

If I couldn't listen to music sober then I'd have to start to learn.

I fucking would now.

Be it maudlin, artificial, guilt-induced . . . grieve I would.

You listen to Johnny Cash and it doesn't move you, you're already in rigor mortis. Turned the music up – Johnny in full gravel. I surveyed my apartment. The new music centre, when did I get that? Or where? The bookshelves lined with volumes, courtesy of Vinny . . . how'd that happen?

You can operate in a blackout and be sober, the legacy of the years of waste. You can stop drinking but never get clear. As I assessed my domain, I mouthed aloud,

'Adds up to what?'

The Dandy Warhols, why did they pop into my head? The adrenalin was cruising, opening the Information Highway in my mind. A deluge of useless data came flooding out – a passage I'd memorized during my training at Templemore:

On 17 August 1922, a contingent of the Civic Guard under the command of Chief Superintendent Mattias McCarthy, having occupied Dublin Castle, lined up in the lower castle yard for inspection by Eamonn Duggan TD, Minister for Home Affairs.

The *Irish Times* the next day reported, 'Yesterday's little ceremony removes the last trace of the old regime . . . Ireland's destinies are in Irish hands. If the new Ireland is served by a force which will uphold the best traditions of the Royal Irish Constabulary she will be fortunate indeed.'

My early days of training, I'd memorized those words as a source of pride. They bore witness to the career I was going to honour and bring credit to. I remember having the *Irish Times* piece on the wall of my room. It lightened my heart every time I read it, made me feel I was part of the country, a tangible power for the betterment of the nation.

Jesus.

The CD finished.

Shook my head, knew if I looked in the mirror I would see tombstones in my eyes. Was listening to music to bring oblivion and what I got was the dead. All my own people, and for some reason those I'd never even known. James Furlong, the Sky war correspondent, filed one bogus report after a lifetime of real dangerous reporting and couldn't live with the shame. That his Down Syndrome daughter found him hanging tore me to shreds. I asked God,

'Where's the fucking joy You promise? Where's the happy times I've been obsessing about?'

The list of deceased continued. A Righteous Brother, June Carter and David Hemmings, who'd been in Galway in the late sixties to star in *Alfred the Great*, fresh from his triumph in *Blow-Up* and then the sexiest man on the planet. The movie was described as the greatest turkey of its time, but was welcome in the city due to the income it generated.

Stood, willing myself to shed the shadows, selected REM . . . *Best of* compilation, track six, 'Losing My Religion', about him being in the corner.

I was moving, doing Stipe's routine. How sad is that? A man in his fifties, the debris of a ruined life dogging his memory, dancing on the top floor of an apartment over Galway Bay, knowing every word of the song, thinking,

Boilermaker.

Bourbon with a beer chaser, living some distorted idea of the American dream.

Another gulp of self pity, another disc.

Springsteen with 'Thunder Road'. Nick Hornby estimated he played the song 1,500 times.

What . . . he was counting?

Shouted the refrain, something about no free ride.

Like I didn't know.

Then, like a classic crime story, 'Meeting Across The River', the line in there about carrying a gun as if it was a friend.

Then I sat in the chair, surveyed the empty apartment, the ghosts of all I'd ever known. Jeez, was suicide such a bad idea?

Getting there.

Bruce finished with the Tom Waits song 'Jersey Girl' and I sang along, quieter now, near weeping for a Jersey girl I'd never encountered and never would, not ever. And did the thing drunks always regret, swear they will never do, but it's, like, compulsory. Picked up the phone, some soul loneliness begging for a human voice, rapped in the digits, heard Ridge go,

'Yes?'

Tentative.

I said,

'It's Jack.'

No warm cry of welcome.

So I added,

'You won't have any more trouble.'

Stunned.

'You found him?'

'Yes.'

'And who . . . is he?'

'Name of Sam White. You did him for public urination.'

I was happy with the turn of phrase, only slightly slurred on the Sam. The Ss are a bastard, get you every time when you're in such a state of agitation. I must have sounded like I was drunk.

She was rummaging in her memory, then,

'Him! He's the one?'

'Not any more.'

'Did you hurt him?'

'Yes.'

'How badly?'

'Biblical.'

I waited, wondering if she'd go nuts, accuse me of being a vigilante, ask me what I thought the Guards were for. She said,

'Good.'

I expected a show of gratitude, at least some appreciation, but she went,

'You sound odd.'

'Yeah? Funny thing about violence, it puts your gift for small talk down the toilet.'

'Were you hurt?'

'Not any place that it shows.'

She savoured this, then,

'What does that mean?'

I could have given her the talk on how violence takes a bit of your soul, that damaging another person diminishes your humanity, but there was no way of saying that without sounding like a prick, so I said,

'You're smart, you'll figure it out.'

Steel in her voice, she said,

'Don't take that tone with me.'

Crashed the phone down.

God does not help those who help the Guards.

In my head was the speech Clare had given me, the condescension he'd shown me, the names he called me, and I was forced to unclench my fingers where they'd burned into a tight fist. Last time I was that angry, I punched a hole in the wall and broke my wrist.

*　*　*

Noon the following day, I met Malachy in the Great Southern. He had a pot of coffee going, a cloud of nicotine over his head. He said,

'Christ, you look rough.'

I'd needed a pot of coffee to get up and out, snapped,

'What's it to you?'

He considered that. I took one of his cigarettes and he managed not to comment. I realized I still had the patch on so I put the cig back in the pack. Without preamble, I laid out the investigation as it happened, from meeting the bouncer guy to Michael Clare's admission of killing Father Joyce. I didn't say I didn't believe the story. Finished, I sat back, asked,

'What are you going to do?'

'Do?'

'He murdered your friend, a priest . . . will you go to the Guards?'

He shook the coffee pot empty, said,

'I'll say a Mass for him.'

I couldn't believe it, asked,

'You're kidding, right?'

He was looking at his diary, making *hmmm* sounds, said,

'The early-morning Mass, at seven. Will you come?'

I stood up, went,

'So Clare walks, that it?'

He had an expression of what I can only describe as resigned tolerance, not one I'd ever seen him display. He said,

''Tis God's business now.'

I wanted to reach down, grab him by his clerical collar

and shake him till he rattled. I said,

'Clare told me of an unholy trinity of the Church, the Guards and him. He should have added you – you don't seem to care if he's the guilty one or not, you just want to know if your arse is safe.'

He sighed.

'Jack, those men, they have a vision of the future. Small people like you and me, we go along, they can see the bigger picture.'

I wanted to beat him senseless. I stood up, and for the first time in my life I wanted to spit on someone, bring up a ton of phlegm and gob it out on his tired suit. You're about to spit on a priest, you're so fucked, even the Devil is mildly taken aback. I managed to rein it in and said,

'I'd say God forgive you, but I think even He would see that as a reach. You're one sad wanker, and you know what? I think you interfered with those boys too.'

And I was out of there. Jeff's pub, Nestor's, was only a few hundred yards away and it was so appealing to head there. I looked at Eyre Square, the winos congregating, whispered,

'Where are you, buddy?'

I was nursing a diet coke in Feeney's when Cody arrived. I put my fingers to my lips, said,

'No comment on the diet coke. You don't know me well enough to have an opinion, least not one that matters a shit to me.'

He took a deep breath, said,

'My father always treated me like a retarded person, said

I'd never come to anything, that I was a fierce disappointment, and you know, you made me feel like I was *someone*.'

His voice faltered and I thought he was going to cry, but
he bit down, held it together, sort of, continued,

'This sounds stupid, and I know it's, like, weird, but I
thought you were kind of like the father I'd have wanted.'

Before I could respond, he said in a rush,

'But I can't stomach the rage, the ferocity you have, so
I resign. I'm afraid I'll end up like you.'

I wanted to shout,

'*Resign?* Are you fucking kidding me?'

He stood up, said,

'Goodbye, and . . . am, God bless.'

I watched him shuffle out, and I swear to God, it looked
like he had a limp.

18

*'They throw earth over your head
and it is finished for ever.'*

Pascal, *Pensées*, 210

That night will remain as one of the strangest of my strange life. I made strong coffee, real bright idea if you want to sleep, and man, I wanted to sleep for ever. But the music, the mania of violence and remorse had gotten a hold, so I played every sad song I had, and I had a whole bunch. The caffeine fuelled my madness and I swear, I think the whole emotional storm, the barrage of pure feeling caused me to hallucinate.

I saw my father outside the window, holding Serena May in his arms.

Imagine how I'd have been if I'd drunk, if that was the reaction on just coffee, albeit gallons of it. Come five in the morning, my stomach roared *enough* and I threw up, then, knackered, fell on the bed and slept like a demented animal.

I came to in the morning, sick as a tinker in the belly of the beast. My clothes stank to high heaven and I'd that emotional hangover that recovering alcoholics discuss. One thing they got right, it's a bastard. Already I missed Cody. That kid – Jesus, I nearly said *my kid* – had got to me, and

I could at least attempt to put that right. But then and there, what I needed was a shower, *no coffee* and a lot of prayer.

I had entered a realm of pure madness. The place where you actually believe you are sane. There was a pounding on the door, not a polite knocking but a definite heavy banging. Man, I was ready to rumble unless it was the Guards. Pulled the door open.

When I first came to the building, one of the residents had stopped me, warned,

'This is a quiet residence.'

I'd been enraged. Here he was again. About thirty, wearing a buttoned green cardigan, a shirt and tie, heavy dark pants and slippers, metal glasses that gave him a Nazi look. I said,

'What?'

He took a step back. My appearance was not encouraging. The rumpled blazer, dirty pants, and no doubt eyes of lunacy. He put his hand to his tie for reassurance, said,

'The level of noise from your apartment last night is not acceptable.'

I grabbed his tie, hauled him to me, snarled,

'Who the fuck are you?'

Flecks of spittle landed on his cardigan. He was horrified, glanced at the phlegm on his shoulder, stammered,

'I'm Tony Smith. I head up the Residents' Committee.'

Pricks like him had shadowed my whole life. Always they'd a committee or organization to hide behind. My breath was clouding his glasses. I hissed,

'Get off my fucking back. Since the day I moved in, you've been reading me the riot act. Now here's a riot. I ever see you again, I'll break every fucking bone in your body . . . and if you think of calling the Guards . . .'

I paused, not so much for effect – though it helped – but mainly to catch my breath, then,

'I used to be a Guard and we watch out for our own.'

I released his tie and he staggered back. I said,

'You ever pound on my door again, you better be carrying more than an attitude. Now piss off.'

Slammed the door in his miserable face, my chest heaving from adrenalin and palpitations. In the kitchen, I got a glass of water, drained half. I was way out on an avalanche of madness.

Why?

Because I'd gone certifiably insane. Because Michael Clare bothered me, bothered me a lot. If I'd been calmer, I'd have, as they say, *sucked it up* – swallowed the bile and moved on. Not now.

The phone rang. I picked up, went,

'Yeah?'

'Jack, it's Ridge.'

'So?'

That was the spirit, take the war to her too. She was momentarily lost for a reply, then,

'Are you all right?'

'Never better. This might be the bloody best I've ever been.'

Outrage in her voice as she came back.

'You're drinking. Oh Holy Mother of God, I can't believe it.'

'Hey, God has nothing to do with it, this is purely a deal

with the Devil, and whether you believe it or not, I haven't
been drinking. I was going to, came within a glass of it,
but no, I didn't drink . . . Hurrah for me, eh?'

She gave a deep sigh then, almost resigned, said,

'We'll have to get you some help.'

That inflamed me – not that it took a whole lot to fire
me up. I echoed,

'We! Who's *we*? You're the same as me, Ridge – we don't
have anybody. But *you* can do something.'

'Tell me.'

'Mind your own business.'

And for once, I got to slam the phone down.

An alkie in full defiant flight is a wonder to behold. Like a
victim of a car wreck who straight away runs out into traffic.
The rage is usually short lived, and I'd been burning adrenalin and aggression for over an hour, full-tilt boogie. I
suddenly collapsed and climbed into bed, torn blazer and
all.

The next few days were nightmare in neon, highlit by
dread, punctuated by pain. A blur of waking and sleeping,
massive sweats, ice-cold shivers and the odd hallucination,
but no booze. Weak as a kitten, I managed to wash, dress,
gulp food down without even tasting it. Tacked the menu
of bare survival on the back of the door: eat, drink gallons
of water, wash, stay enraged.

More than anything else, it demonstrates a life of pure
futility.

I'd like to say it worked, that I'd found a method to not
drink and function.

I hadn't.

Living alone is a huge factor on the road to madness –
who can disapprove? As long as I kept away from mirrors,
I could move in a world of delusion. No easy task to shave
with your eyes averted from your reflection.

So I packed that in.

I needed milk and went across the road to a small shop
that was barely hanging in there, the developers squeezing
tight on all sides. The guy behind the counter was wearing
a turban. More and more, the Irish were sinking into the
background. We didn't speak but eyed each other with a
wary suspicion. I was going to ask,

'Are the people treating you well?'

But I didn't want to know. We were treating our own
like shite so why would we stretch for a non-national? In
the hospitals, patients were lying for days on trolleys, and
this at a time when we'd been declared the fourth-richest
nation in the world. An elderly man came into the shop,
bought one of the tabloids and nodded at me. I grunted,
no encouragement given.

As I left the shop, he caught up with me, said,

'You're the Taylor fella?'

I was primed for aggravation, asked,

'So?'

If he detected my hostility, he wasn't fazed by it, said,

'I saw you recently with that young man. Is he your son?'

Jesus.

And I said,

'Yes, yes he is.'

He gave a huge smile, said,

'Well, he's the spitting image of you.'

And was gone.

The weirdest thing of all – I felt delighted.

Go figure.

But back to the apartment and the continuing dementia.

Knew I looked like shit. Now I could look like shit with a beard.

At infrequent times, I'd let loose a cackle of demented laughter, and that scared the bejaysus out of me. When you frighten yourself, you've hit a planet of new darkness.

I took to muttering 'Michael Clare', like a cursed mantra. It cranked me when the booze compulsion seemed overwhelming. Somewhere in my sick mind – and fevered it was – I equated his exposure with atonement for the death of the child. In jangled sleep, more than once Cathy and Jeff came to me, intoning, 'Baby-killer.'

The destruction of Michael Clare wouldn't bring the little girl back or restore Jeff, but one area of darkness might, and I stress might, contain less shadows.

I began to research my quarry in the library, found old newspapers and, after hours of poring over them, found him featured many times. He was a patron of the Arts and seen often at charity functions. Most importantly, I discovered he had a sister, Cathleen, known as Kate. She was single, living in Salthill, apart from that I couldn't find a whole lot more about her. So I figured, cold call, why the hell not? Bought some clothes from Age Concern and I was ready to roll. A light-blue suit, white T-shirt and soft-soled shoes. My limp was acting up something ferocious. It had to be related to the anger, what wasn't? Had an energy drink, some shite that promised to restore your spiritual and physical balance, and decided to walk out there. The sea air would do me some good and get some wind on my face. I took the Grattan Road route and a few people said hello, but I pretended not to hear them. I remembered the bouncer guy saying he walked the prom and never spoke to a single soul. I understood better now. Half expected to meet him, but it didn't happen.

Kate lived in a new apartment block beside the Blackrock Tower. The building looked flash, expensive, a list of names beside the intercom. There she was: K. Clare. It was too dangerous now to use a woman's Christian name on such a list. Sign of the disintegrating times. I rang the bell and after a moment heard a woman's voice.

'Yes?'

'I'm sorry to bother you, but I'd like to talk to you about your brother Michael. If you give Tom Reed a call, he'll vouch for me. My name is Jack Taylor.'

Silence, and I thought, nope, not going to work. Then,

'Are you the man who saved the swans?'

Jesus, that was a time ago. My picture had been in the paper and I got an award for my valour. It was most embarrassing and hugely unwarranted. I said,

'Am, yeah.'

The intercom buzzed and the door opened. Her apartment was on the second floor and she was waiting at the door, a smile in place. Tall, she was in the late-forties zone that in some light passes for mid-thirties, mainly due to grooming, care and cash.

The very first thing I noticed was her hands, unnaturally

large for a woman and rough, like she'd been washing dishes all her life, which I seriously doubted. She caught my look, said,

'I'm ashamed of them, but as I work with horses they have their use. You need to have very strong hands to hold a horse that does not want to be held.'

Later, I read all sorts of meaning into that. Then, I let it slide.

Black hair to her shoulders, a navy dress that hugged her frame in the best way and a face that was just an inch away from ordinary. She extended her hand, said,

'I'm glad to meet the saviour of the swans.'

I took her hand, felt the strength and decided to let her believe I was heroic. She waved me inside, and the first thing I saw were framed photos of the swans in the Claddagh Basin, shot from every angle. One in particular was highly effective, at dusk, the swans taking on an almost mystical quality. I said,

'Wow.'

She laughed, agreed,

'Beautiful creatures.'

The apartment was simply but elegantly furnished, taste and money giving a comfortable, relaxed atmosphere. She indicated an armchair and I sat. She was nervous and I realized how long it had been since I'd found any woman even vaguely appealing. I had totally shut down that part of my life, never expecting to even miss those feelings. On a small table near me was a tiny silver swan, exquisitely made, every feature outlined. It seemed almost real. She said,

'One of a pair.'

She gazed at it, then,

'I had it made by a craftsman in Quay Street. Actually, I had a pair done. Did you know swans mate for life, are inseparable?'

The obvious question of why this one was alone was on my lips, but she got there before me, said,

'I gave the other to . . . Well, I gave it away. A mistake, I now realize, but at the time it seemed . . . appropriate.'

She asked,

'Can I get you a drink?'

Making it easy for me. So I said,

'Perhaps a glass of water.'

She said she might have a little touch of whiskey and sparkling water, that normally she didn't much care for alcohol. I had to stifle the scream that went, *Shut the fuck up! Drink it, don't drink it, but for Chrissakes stop talking about it.* I gave a polite smile – the one that says, 'Oh, we all have our little vices.'

She held up a bottle of Black Bushmills and I nearly caved. Christ, the cream of booze, goes down like a dream. She said,

'Michael would kill me for even suggesting I put water in. He says women don't know how to treat fine whiskey.'

The words *Michael* and *kill* in the same sentence pulled me back to why I was there, and I felt a wave of depression hover. She handed me a heavy Waterford tumbler with my water. I raised my glass and said,

'Slainte.'

Got a small smile in return, then she asked,

'About Michael?'

I considered various evasive tactics, but she didn't seem the type to shoot a line to so I said,

'He's been mentioned in connection with the murder of Father Joyce.'

If she was shocked, she hid it well. Her expression didn't change. She placed her glass on a small table, asked,

'And your interest, Mr Taylor? You're not here in any official capacity, I think.'

Her voice was like Michael's, a touch of English accent but a more cultured sound. I said,

'My role is to eliminate Tom Reed and Michael from the inquiry.'

Her eyes held mine and she said,

'Are you employed by someone?'

Now I had to lie, went,

'The Church is anxious to get former altar boys cleared so as not to sully their already tarnished image in the eyes of the public.'

I thought it sounded pretty plausible. Her eyes stayed on mine, which I was finding disconcerting. She asked,

'Have you met with Michael?'

I said I had and that he had been most cooperative. She stood up, sighed, said,

'I doubt that very much, Mr Taylor.'

Caught me off balance, and before I could respond she added,

'Michael is . . . troubled. I think it's the oldest story in the book – fathers and sons. He wanted so much to impress my father, but alas, he never did, and the tragedy is, he's still trying. He believes if he drags this city into massive

prosperity, my father will finally approve. My father has
been dead for twenty years.'

I raised my glass to buy time, took a decent wallop and
felt the sheer smoothness rush down my throat, said,

'Do you have contact with him?'

She ran her hand through her hair, looked out the
window, which had a fine view of the bay, said,

'We lost Michael when he was ten years old, when . . .
that . . . priest destroyed him. To our shame, we never
believed him. My mother actually beat him ferociously for
telling the truth – we're as guilty as that . . . *cleric* . . . for
what he's become. Michael and I were joined at the hip
almost as children, went everywhere together, did everything together, but our big treat was to feed the swans.
We'd spend hours there, fascinated by those wondrous creatures.'

Then she sat, said,

'I don't know why I'm telling you this. Maybe because
you saved the swans or maybe I just needed to say it. Those
silver swans, I had them made for Michael's twenty-first, a
last desperate effort to connect with him. He returned them
to me, said he hated those bloody things.'

A thought struck and I said,

'But he has his office overlooking the Claddagh Basin. If
he hates them, surely that's the last place he'd set up?'

She sighed, then,

'He bought out his partner who was originally estab-
lished there. It made good commercial sense to remain.
Anyway, Michael doesn't see them. Since he was ten years
old, he sees different things to you and I.'

I had to ask, so plunged.

'What do you think he sees?'

She considered.

'I think he sees our father, the stern look. My father hated priests, he strongly objected to Michael being an altar boy, but it was my mother's wish. Irish women and priests . . .'

She let that trail off and I could have said,

'Fucking tell me about it. My own mother and that scumbag Malachy.'

Instead I visualized Michael.

I recalled the time I visited him, and him standing at the window as I left, his eyes like panes of glass, looking inwards.

Her glass was empty and I asked if she'd like me to get her another. She said,

'No, it's no solution.'

I could have told her a few stories from that war zone to reinforce her comment. I decided to tell her the truth, said,

'Michael told me he killed Father Joyce.'

Her eyes were back on mine and full of such sorrow that I wanted to hold her, but of course I just sat there and she said,

'You want me to confirm if it could be true, am I right, Mr Taylor? That's why you're here.'

I wanted to scream that yes, that's what brought me, but fuck Michael, fuck them all. I wanted to give up the fight, they were too powerful. Her voice almost a whisper, so I had to lean forward to hear her, she said,

'Let me tell you a story, Mr Taylor. Three boys, molested

by a priest, become adults, and together they get the strength to accuse this man, this religious icon, of abusing them. Then Michael becomes this high-powered businessman, a vital figure in the community, and golfs with the leaders of society. He has to change his image, at least outwardly.'

She stopped, looked up for a moment as if she was hearing something, perhaps the voice of a ten-year-old boy, then added,

'But no matter how much you seem to change, I don't imagine you can ever quite escape the past.'

Nothing further. I asked,

'You think Michael . . .'

She cut me off, said,

'Our family were great hunters. Do you shoot, Mr Taylor?'

Of all the questions I was expecting, that one was not on the list. What do you say to it? That when you're raised in poverty, the only shooting you get to do is the penny arcade. I was going to suggest she maybe could give Cathy some lessons, help her get that aim up, show her how to shoot high, but instead went with,

'No, it's not one of my accomplishments.'

Let a little bitterness leak over the words and she caught it. Her eyes did a little dance, then she said,

'I shoot, Mr Taylor, and at competition level. If anyone were to hurt my Michael, I wouldn't hesitate to hunt them down, like the vermin I'd consider them.'

I nearly laughed. Was she threatening me? Then she let out a small sigh, said,

'I think you should go, Mr Taylor. I'm tired.'

A small fire was glowing in the grate. It lent an air of cosiness to the room that was definitely bogus. I clocked neat piles of cut logs beside the fire, and a small axe. I was going to ask if she cut the wood herself. She moved to the flames, added a log, and while she was doing so, I don't know why, I swiped the swan. Call it an act of defiance, a moment of sheer impetuousness, or maybe just theft.

At the door, I tried to find words to defer the departure, but nothing came. I was going to go bold, ask,

'Michael ever borrow your little axe?'

But I was in the corridor and she closed the door.

Very quietly.

19

'Expectation is one of the great sources of suffering.'

Buddhist saying

Found a new pub. From necessity, it would have to be one that existed below the radar. I'd often heard about Coyle's, at the arse end of Dominic Street. It was almost an urban myth, had a rep. beyond salvage. The rumour was, it never closed, merely shut the doors come midnight, kept the bodies on an even keel. Come early morning, the doors opened and a dawn batch of the living dead entered. The only requirement was money. Fights, brawls, derangement were accepted. What wasn't accepted was civility or citizenship, in the sense of being a pillar of the community or belonging to the community in any fashion.

It was the last port of call before the street or the grave.

When I washed up there, no one objected. An empty stool at the counter with, if not my name on it, then certainly my condition.

Welcome to hell.

My first session there, I recognized a few faces, the faces of the disappeared. Guys I knew at school, guys I'd grown up with and presumed dead. In a way they were. As I ordered a large whiskey, a few of them waved, if weakly.

I heard *Jack . . . Taylor*, and perhaps imagined, *What kept you?* The barman/owner, called Trade, had been a boxer and looked like he lost each and every fight. The nickname was due to his trading anything, anyone, anytime, for money. He wasn't in business to make friends, be popular, his sole concern was money.

Bald, big, with dead yellow eyes, he looked at me, said,

'We have one brand of whiskey, a house brand. You OK with that?'

House translates as no brand, to rot gut. I nodded, laid some bills on the counter and he poured, put it in front of me. I had a shake in my hand but that was mandatory. I knew if I took a slug it would catapult me off the stool, 100 per cent proof and tasting like turpentine. He asked,

'That to your liking?'

The sheer proximity of the alcohol had momentarily robbed me of speech and he said,

'Like you give a shit about taste.'

I swear he chuckled as he moved off. It was said poteen was added to the mix and I was a believer. A dense cloud of smoke hovered above and the walls were yellow from nicotine. The new anti-smoking ban in pubs etc. wouldn't be having a whole lot of impact here. I chanced a look around, saw an ex-Guard, but he wasn't seeing anything, he had the punched-out expression of one who is not responding to any count. Moved from the stool. A chair was vacant beside a beat-up table and I took that. Seemed to me that the atmosphere was similar to the asylum, the same sense of blunted despair. A guy across from me asked,

'How you doing?'

His tone had a hint of challenge. I looked at him, taking my time, not doing anything too quickly. He could have been twenty or sixty, his eyes were out of focus. I said,

'Not bad.'

Seemed to take that as an invitation, rolled up a chair and joined me, said,

'I've a gambling problem.'

I nearly laughed but held it back, nodded solemnly. He indicated a man in the corner, asked,

'See him?'

I thought of the REM song.

I warranted I did and, still staring at the man, he said,

'Used to be a priest.'

I nearly asked,

'What happened?'

But if ever a question was redundant. The guy laughed, a high-pitched titter, not quite hysteria but as close as you'd get without howling, said,

'Used to be . . . that's what you get here.'

No fighting that. He stared at me, an edge creeping into his voice, asked,

'So what's your story, what used you to be?'

His body had tensed. In a split second he'd gone from amiable to aggressive. I asked, letting a little hard leak into my own voice,

'It matter?'

He laughed out loud, then abruptly stood up as if he heard some call to arms and marched out with singular purpose.

When I was leaving a time later, Trade said,

'You didn't touch your drink.'

Sounded almost friendly. I asked,

'You're open during the night?'

He gave me a long look and I wondered if I'd crossed some invisible boundary. He said,

'Tell you what, you're passing in the middle of the night, knock on the door, see what happens. That answer your question?'

I nodded and got out of there.

That night I dreamt of my father. He was sitting in his chair in the kitchen, weeping, weeping, no words, only a silent woeful crying. I woke up – it disturbed me more than your out-and-out nightmare. He was a strong man in every sense of the word, and I don't remember him being afraid of anything. Not that he was some type of macho asshole, but he faced whatever life threw at him without any fuss. Whatever came down the pike, he was, if not ready for it, at least willing to meet it. Like everyone, though, he had his area of vulnerability, some odd quirk that made sense only to him. His was the back door. We lived in a terraced council house with a small garden at the rear. My mother was a fresh-air fiend. She was a fiend full stop, but fresh air was one of her favourite methods of irritation. The depths of winter, she'd have all the windows open and God help you if you closed one. My father suffered that in silence, as he did most of her actions, but the back door was the exception. It drove him crazy to see it open. It's the only irrational act of his I ever saw. My mother, of course, was forever opening it and he'd straight away close it. One of those little scenes of brooding warfare that marriage entails, conducted without words but laden with intent. An evening, she was at the rosary in the church and she'd opened the door prior to her departure. As soon as she left he hopped up, didn't quite slam it but certainly closed it with force. I always had a great relationship with him, could talk to him and ask him questions and he never cut me short. I realize now that it was a blessing of rare stature. That evening, I asked,

'Why do you need the door closed?'

He used to smoke then, not a lot, just a few Woodbines after work. If he finished a ten pack in a week, it was pushing it. He took out the packet, slowly extracted one, lit it with a kitchen match, the long ones, shaped like tapers. I can still recall the aroma of the cigarette and the sulphur, it seemed like the scent of safety. He looked at me, said,

'You leave the back door open, rodents will come in.'

And I nearly laughed. That's what I remember most, suppressing that bubbling urge to guffaw, and I thank God a thousand times that I didn't. He was so solemn and I realized he was deadly serious. We never mentioned it again.

The night after my father's burial, some neighbours had been in, drinking Jameson, eating fruit cake, reminiscing about him. I was sent to bed right after they left. As I lay there, numb with the loss of him, I heard my mother throw open the back door and I hated her with a fierce passion. I must have dozed, as I heard her screaming as if from a distance, then sat up and she was roaring like a banshee. I took my time going down. She was standing on a hard chair, a look of terror on her face. She shrieked,

'There's a rat, the biggest rat I ever saw. He ran in – I think he's under the table.'

I pretended to poke about, but mainly what I did was shut the door, loudly. I came round to look at her on the chair and she asked,

'Is it gone?'

I threw my eyes towards the door, said,

'I don't see it.'

Then I went up to bed. I don't know how long she stayed down there, nor do I care. All I know is the back door stayed permanently shut. Shortly after that, I bought my first pack of Woodbines, the ten size. I don't have any moral or wisdom to draw from that event, all I know is that, like my dad said, sooner or later the vermin show up.

I am, of course, aware that some might say that, one way or another, I've been shutting doors ever since.

A state of mind that could only be described as savage, somewhere in the literature of recovery that is used to describe the dry alcoholic. 'Tis sad, 'tis true.

I was in my apartment, trying to shed the remnants of the dream about my father. A loud howl of anguish had awakened me. I'd sat up, terror in my soul, wondering what on earth was happening to some poor fucker to make them emit such a sound, then felt the tears on my cheeks and realized the person who'd made the cry was me. I don't think distress gets more awful than that.

I was carrying the tiny swan in my pocket like some dumb talisman. I decided to pay a return visit to Tom Reed, the bouncer. He'd been fairly receptive and I wanted to see how he'd react to Michael Clare's admission of guilt. If anyone knew Michael, it had to be Tom.

En route, I bought some coffee, milk, biscuits. As I approached his house, I could hear the phones shrilling, so business was still hectic. Rang the bell and the same harried girl answered. I said,

'This time I brought supplies.'

She waved me in and rushed to answer a phone. Tom was in the kitchen, and if he appreciated the shopping, he didn't say. I said,

'Hope you don't mind, but I just wanted to run a few things by you.'

He looked tired, said,

'And a carton of milk, some biscuits, they entitle you to what?'

His tone was borderline hostile, so I tried,

'To a cup of coffee, maybe?'

No response.

I attempted that bad cliché they use in movies.

'If this is a bad time?'

Didn't fly.

He sighed, letting out a suppressed breath, asked,

'And a good time would be when?'

Before I could counter with some lame reply, he said accusingly,

'You went to see Kate.'

'Am, yes. Was that not a good idea?'

He was wearing a white shirt that needed a wash – many washes – and navy pants that were too wide in the waist. He pulled at them but it made little difference. I didn't know how to get this on a friendlier level, said,

'I walked the prom, thought I might run into you.'

He snapped,

'I don't do that shit any more, I've a business to run.'

Then he seemed to weigh something in his head.

'Kate and I have some history.'

I kept my face neutral, said,

'Terrific woman.'

Now he began to make coffee, boiled the kettle, spooned heaps of granules into mugs, added the water, handed a mug to me and indicated I should sit. During all this frenzied activity, he didn't speak and I was content to wait. He took a sip of his coffee, then,

'Damaged as I was, I was really prepared to make a go of it, but she was obsessed with someone else.'

What do you say, *Bummer*? I nodded and he said,

'How do you have a relationship when the woman is in love with her brother?'

Oh.

He continued,

'As kids they were inseparable. You couldn't get closer than those two. Then Father Joyce began his . . .'

He floundered for a word and I wanted to help out, the way it is when you're with someone who stammers but you know you'd better not. He finally settled for,

'. . . Activities, and Michael was lost to her, to everyone. She has never stopped trying to get his attention back – is that the saddest fucking thing you ever heard? Years later, when we hooked up, it was only so she could maybe get a way to be with Michael. Her other passion, horses, she loves them, saw her bring down a wild mare one time. Her hands, did you notice them? Jesus, I'd have given me soul to have touched them.'

He seemed broken and his attention had rooted in the past. To jolt him back, I said,

'Michael told me he did Father Joyce. Do you think he did?'

The possibility didn't faze him. He thought about it, then said,

'He's capable of it – shit, I'm capable of it – but my instinct says he didn't.'

My scepticism of his instinct must have shown and he said,

'Plus, years ago, when Michael and I were using booze to get by – oh yeah, we drank together – we spent an evening contemplating that very thing, killing the fucker, and discussing how we'd do it. I said I'd burn him, yeah, let him feel hell, as I've done for all the years, but Michael said he'd drown him, because he robbed him of the swans, the love of water. The Claddagh Basin, that's where he'd bring him, let him die beside the very animals he'd stolen from him.'

I thought of how close I'd come to burning the stalker, the look on Cody's face after. Tom rubbed his face as if this whole trip down memory lane was the most exhausting thing he'd done in years, and maybe it was, said,

'You're really taking this seriously.'

I admitted it had got a hold on me, I couldn't shake it till I knew the answer. He asked,

'You talk to Sister Mary Joseph?'

'Who?'

'I didn't want to mention her because, despite everything, I always kind of liked her. But she was Joyce's housekeeper, secretary, woman of all trades and she knew, she knew what he was doing and stayed quiet. I often wonder how she squares that now.'

'Where would I find her?'

He seemed to find that a stupid question, said,

'At the church, where else? Unless she's dead, but I think I'd have known if she was. Yeah, go see her, she's the one who knows where the bodies are, if you'll excuse the pun. Bring her some ice cream, she'd a thing for that.'

He'd a small smile at the corner of his mouth as he said that and I marvelled at his forgiveness, said,

'I'm amazed at your ability to forgive her. That is really something.'

His eyes flared and he asked,

'Did I say I forgave her? I hate the fucking bitch. With any luck, she's turned to drink.'

He stood up, said,

'One more thing. It's odd, but then what isn't?'

He seemed to have a struggle as to whether to divulge it, then,

'Kate, she loves those swans, does all kinds of work to ensure their safety, but . . . she is also a hunter.'

I wasn't following, asked,

'She hunts swans?'

And got a look of total irritation. He snapped,

'Don't be so bloody stupid, course not the swans. She shoots pheasants and any other wildlife that moves.'

I didn't believe him, stammered,

'I don't . . . am . . . believe you.'

He gave me a deep serious stare, then exclaimed,

'By Christ, you're stupid. Are you sure you're in the right line of work? This is a woman who cuts her own wood, for fuck's sake. She is the real thing, a primitive, and yes, she hunts. Next time you go visit and you want to get her attention, ask her to show you her rifle, watch her light up.'

He let out his breath. His face had gone grey, the effort of this explanation had taken its toll. I asked,

'You need a shot of brandy or something?'

Hoping he did and maybe I could join him. He shook his head, then sneered,

'You look like you want to hit the sauce your own self.'

The interview or whatever the hell we were having was over. I tried,

'Yeah, well, it's been a rough time.'

And hated myself for even trying to justify it, especially to a person like Tom. He walked me to the door and as I said goodbye he gave me a long look. I figured he was going to suggest AA or say something sympathetic. He said,

'Go to the Claddagh Basin, it's quicker.'

More rattled than I wanted to admit, I headed for my afternoon pit stop, went to Coyle's. Trade nodded as he saw me, didn't say anything, just poured a large whiskey, pushed it down the counter. I laid the money beside the glass and went to take a seat, to move away from him. I really didn't need any more bitterness that day and one thing you could rely on, Trade would be bitterness with ferocity.

Found myself beside the ex-priest and thought, *Oh shit*, and was about to move when he stirred, said,

'Could you kick my right leg?'

I thought I heard him wrong. I echoed,

'Kick your right leg?'

'Yes, please, it's gone to sleep, there's no feeling there.'

His voice had a strangulated quality, the result of surgery or cigarettes or both. I gave his leg a gentle kick and he shook his head. I was aware of how crazy my life had become. I'm sitting in a pub, kicking a priest, and worse, because he asked me. Gave a harder one and he nodded, said,

'Yes, it's coming back.'

He had a face that had been massacred by time, deep ridges on the cheeks, sunken eyes, a grey pallor that had death all over it. His eyes, beneath the red, were once blue, now haunted. He asked,

'Might I buy you a refreshment?'

Jesus, where did he think we were, the carnival? I said I was good and he stretched out a trembling hand, liver spots covering the skin, said,

'I'm Gerald.'

I took the hand. The skin felt light as parchment. I shook it gently, said,

'I'm Jack.'

Before him was a full glass of the house brand and a pack of Players. He gave a wheezing cough, said,

'They'll have told you I was a priest.'

It was hard to hear him and I had to lean forward, a scent of woodsmoke and eau de cologne emanating from him, with booze of course in there. I admitted that yes, they had, and he said,

'They tell the newcomers. I think they like to show me off.'

He gave a tiny smile as if he was the most amused. He tried to reach for the cigarettes but failed, so I helped him out, got one fired up for him. He asked if I wished for one. I said I was still on the patches and laughed myself, adding,

'Here I am at the end of the road and trying to stop smoking.'

He gave that deep consideration, or else he had gone to sleep, then he asked,

'Do you believe in evil, Jack?'

I looked round to see if we could be heard, but no one was paying any attention so I said,

'I've seen it first hand.'

He turned to face me, said,

'Yes, yes you have. And did it burn you?'

I told the truth, went,

'It did and it still does.'

He said,

'I was in attendance at an exorcism once.'

I wasn't sure I wanted to hear about that. I had enough demons to carry without getting first-hand testimony on them. He was quiet, then said,

'You surprise me, Jack. Most people would be full of curiosity.'

I measured my words, tried,

'The thing is, if I ask you something, can I live with the answer?'

His face creased in a smile of genuine delight and he said,

'What a wonderful reply. You could be a metaphysician.'

He took a tiny swallow and I ventured,

'Was the exorcism successful?'

The question seemed to trouble him, then,

'The boy had said voices were controlling him. After, he said he was controlling the voices. Would you deem that success?'

Needed some time to digest it, then I said,

'Well, it would certainly be progress, but for whom?'

And as I said it, I realized that only three places were really conducive to such a conversation:

Pubs,

Asylums,

Religious houses.

Gerald raised his right hand, held it there, and it dawned on me he was signalling Trade. I said,

'Hey, I'll get it for you.'

He shook his head, said,

'No need, I'm the only customer he serves at a table and that's because he suffers from fear. He thinks if he cultivates a priest, even a poor excuse for one, he'll be saved, the misguided wretch.'

Sure enough, Trade was over in a flash, asking in a voice I'd never heard,

'What will it be, Gerald?'

'Two of your finest, innkeeper – one for my comrade.'

Trade gave me an odd look, as if he'd misjudged me, went to get the drinks. My first one stood untouched, like original sin. Gerald said,

'The demon spoke to me at that exorcism. You wish to know what it said?'

I figured I could handle it, said,

'Yes.'

'It said it would kill me.'

Not for the first time, I jumped to the wrong conclusion, asked,

'Is that why you ended up here?'

He gave a full laugh which disintegrated into a bellow of phlegm, then,

'Good Lord, no. The demon is the father of lies. I'm here because of drink.'

Trade was back, put two lethal amounts before us. Gerald produced a wad of notes and Trade took three, said,

'Thank you, Father.'

I moved my glass a few inches, said,

'Cheers.'

He nodded and said,

'The cure of evil is simple, but oh so complicated.'

I was hoping to go, so to speed up the deal asked,

'And it is?'

'Love.'

What a crock. He must have sensed my disappointment, said,

'I've never asked, in my sentence here, never once asked why a person was here, but I'd like to ask you, Jack, if you don't mind?'

Did I mind? Well, maybe a little, but what was there to lose? Said,

'I killed a child.'

He groaned in actual pain, his face contorted and I thought I'd caused a stroke, but he rallied, said,

'What an awesome burden.'

We sat in silence for a while. Not an uncomfortable one, but laden with significance, and finally he said,

'There is an answer.'

I insisted,

'No, Gerald, no there isn't.'

He seemed to expect that and went,

'Forgive yourself, that's the key.'

He disappointed me. What a tired, lousy cliché. I had anticipated better from him, but I suppose he was, after all, just a priest. He said,

'I've disappointed you, yes?'

'A little.'

'I'm truly sorry, I don't have anything else. You're no doubt familiar with the words *Come to me and I will give you rest*. Alas, that's a lie.'

I stood up, said,

'I've got to go. See you another day, maybe.'

His eyes were closing and I saw he was on the verge of sleep. He muttered,

'The Devil's right hand.'

I near scoffed, went,

'Revelations?'

'No, Steve Earle.'

20

'A priest is a wolf in sheep's clothing.'

Old saying

Poets and demons, fathers and sons. The story of my existence, and I don't know if I believed in either. I was coming down Dominic Street, a miserable half-hearted rain beginning, couldn't make up its mind whether to piss heavy or dribble on. There was a time I read Louis McNeice and I knew *Autumn Journal* by heart . . . lines coming to me, like . . . bullets from a forgotten war. Something about haunted faces and the description *surly*.

For a long time, I'd thought *surly* was *hurley* . . . which in light of my recent activities was a whole other weapon. I muttered the lines as I limped along . . . some more exploding in my mind . . . rotten guts . . . I know those words were in there.

Then Cody appeared from the canal side. There's a huge sign saying,

The Samaritans, we're here for you

planted right by the water, so if they couldn't help you, was the river the next stop?

He was nervous, asked,

'Can I speak to you?'

I looked at him, let my body go slack then put out my hand, said,

'I was out of order and I want to . . . apologize.'

His face lit up and he protested I'd nothing to be sorry for, weren't we mates and partners? I was already sorry I'd apologized. He said,

'Jack, she's back.'

He took a deep breath then launched,

'The guy you asked me to look for, Jeff? The wino . . . I mean . . . am . . . your friend. His wife – Cathy? – is back from London, in the Rosin most nights. She gets very drunk, says she's here to shoot you, and she's saying now that you have a son, she can even the tally. What's that about? Do you have a son?'

I ducked the son question and to cover I laughed out loud, said,

'Tell her to join the fucking queue. I already ran into her and it was not . . . conciliatory.'

His mobile rang and he looked sheepish. I said,

'Go ahead, I'll give you a ring later.'

I heard him go,

'Mary *a gra* (love),' and envied him.

I was so glad he was back in my life. I'd nearly said,

'Take care, son.'

Where you turn for O'Brien's Bridge, there's a travel agent's on the corner. I looked in the window: specials to the Canaries, to Barbados, to anywhere. I had to fight down the impulse not to shoot in, book the first available flight to a warm climate and get the fuck out. Pledged to head for America when this whole situation was resolved. I had the money, now all I had to find was the energy.

Tired, a ferocious weariness creeping over me, I headed for my apartment to get some shut eye, try to momentarily forget priests and killers and nuns and ice cream. Gave one of those out-loud laughs that scared the bejaysus out of me as I realized I'd the makings of a country song – to the air of 'Gypsies, Tramps and Thieves' . . .

Had a shower when I got home, made a sandwich of fried rashers, tomato, mayo, built it fat and thick, like the country, and got about as much pleasure from it as the nation was receiving from the numerous tribunals.

Before climbing into bed, I rang Malachy. The phone rang for ages till finally,

'What?'

Gruff, unfriendly, hostile. I asked,

'Is that the way you talk to parishioners?'

'Who's this?'

'Jack Taylor.'

Not happy to hear me. Quelle surprise.

'What do you want?'

Him I could deal with. I said,

'You'd a different tone when your ass was on fire and you wanted a case solved.'

He grunted a bit, then accused,

'You weren't at the Mass.'

'What?'

'I told you I was saying Mass for that poor man who hurt Father Joyce.'

I could hardly believe it, said,

'Hurt? He fucking beheaded him.'

Heard an intake of breath, then,

'Don't use obscenities on the phone.'

This was pointless. I could exchange unpleasantries all day and he'd never tire of it. The clergy have special training for that, they call it theology. I decided to cut to the chase, said,

'I need a favour.'

His tone became heavy with spite, sarcasm.

'By the Holy, the great Jack Taylor wants a favour. I thought you asked no man for quarter?'

Boy, was he being a prick or what? I reined in, asked,

'Could you arrange for me to meet a nun?'

He laughed out loud, went,

'A nun won't save you, boyo.'

If I could have got hold of him . . . Tried,

'Sister Mary Joseph, do you know her?'

'Of course I know her, I'm a priest. How big do you think the town is? This isn't New York yet, we still know our people.'

'Would you arrange a meeting for me?'

I could hear the suspicion in the drawn breath. He snapped,

'Why?'

'I don't know much about Father Joyce, I want to get a fuller picture.'

He snorted. I'm not kidding. I thought that was solely an expression, that only horses actually made that sound, but no, he actually made that awful *snnnnn* . . . Then he said,

'You said the case was closed. The fella confessed, it's over. What are you stirring up trouble for?'

I counted to ten, then,

'If you don't arrange a meeting, I'll kick up such a shit storm, the papers will hear you know the killer and that you . . . what will I say? . . . Yeah, you said a Mass for him. See how the bishop likes to read about you over his poached eggs of a morning.'

I could hear him light a cig. His rage was palpable. He said,

'After the ten o'clock Mass tomorrow morning, I'll bring you to her. And listen, laddie, you better watch your step with her. If I hear you upset her . . .'

Now I laughed, said,

'You have an uncanny resemblance to Clancy, the head honcho of the Guards.'

Malachy changed pitch, said,

'A lovely man. Pity you wouldn't take a page out of his book.'

'Gee, why am I not surprised you and he are buddies?'

He digested that, then took his shot, said,

'Tell your wino *buddies* to stay out of my church. It's not a doss house.'

Got me. I didn't have a clue what he meant, but I had a bad feeling I wasn't going to like it, asked,

'What are you on about?'

'Ha, that fellow with the ponytail you used to knock around with, married to an English wan, kipping down in the door of the church.'

Jeff.

Hit me like thunder. I could hear the tremble in my voice, asked,

'Where did he go?'

Now he was triumphant, said,

'How the devil would I know? I kicked his arse out of there, told him there was a perfectly decent poor house in the Fair Green.'

Click.

Hung up on me. I found the number of the Simon Community in the Fair Green, got through, asked if they had Jeff. They were very helpful, but so many men passed through, they didn't know, and when I described him, they admitted that no, nobody like that had been recently. I rang the hospitals, other shelters – same result. Climbed into bed in black despair.

Up early next morning, got some coffee down, got the fire stoked, kick started the engine which was on very shaky legs. I hate sweet things, but sugar would give me a crank. Showered and assessed the beard progress, without seeing my eyes or most of my face. Required contortions of the frenzied variety. It was shaping up, which was more than I was doing.

Dress for a nun? I knew the key was not to intimidate, to look almost clerical with an air of accountancy. So, the black suit, whitish shirt and tie loosely fastened. I didn't want to seem as if I was collecting for anything. That's their territory. Black shoes that needed polish, so I used spit and a towel. Kind of worked. They weren't great, but at least passable.

The caffeine kicked in. This was only my second day of

being able to drink real coffee – the taste of that decaff is hell on wheels. And I was able to get out the door, the point of the exercise. Went to Roche's, wandered the aisles till I found the ice cream. Shit, what a selection. I hate variety, it confuses me. When I was a child, there was precious little ice cream. Maybe on your First Communion. The choice was vanilla or vanilla. When they added a stick of flake to a cone, there was a huge buzz in the town. Woolworth's had them on special display, titled '99'. I'd asked my father why they were called that and he said that because of the chocolate flake they weren't 100 per cent ice cream. It is probably as good an explanation as any other.

It was all you knew of heaven. I remember pledging that when I grew up I'd live on french fries and 99s. We called fries chips – still do. Everything else is gone to hell in a basket.

As I pondered the dilemma, Liz Hackett came along, a stalwart of Roche's. From Woodquay, she personified all that was best of Galway: friendly, warm, enquiring without being obtrusive. She said,

'Jack Taylor, is it yourself?'

Questions don't come any more Irish or welcoming. I agreed it was and she said,

'I never had you down for an ice-cream lover.'

Which said what?

I nodded, then tried,

'It's not for me, it's for a nun.'

If that sounded as odd to her as it did to me, she hid it well and I asked,

'What flavour would a nun like?'

She looked at the display and asked,

'What order is she?'

I had to check if she was kidding. She wasn't, so I went,

'What difference does that make?'

She adopted a patient tone, as if I wasn't at fault for my ignorance, said,

'Mercy nuns, they like plain. The Presentation ones, they like chocolate, and the enclosed orders, they're not a bit fussy.'

I was staggered, asked,

'How on earth do you know that?'

She gave a resigned smile, said,

'If you're in an enclosed order, ice cream is a very serious business.'

As I had no idea what order Sister Mary Joseph was, I was no more along. I glanced at the American brand, Ben and Jerry's, said,

'Something flashy.'

Liz wasn't so sure, asked,

'Are you absolutely certain?'

I wasn't, but what the hell, what was she going to do . . . complain? And did I give a toss as to whether she enjoyed it or not? Get real.

After some more discussion, Liz said if it was for herself, she'd splurge on Häagen-Dazs, the Strawberry Shortcake, and before I could ask, she added,

'The makers, they were trying to come up with an exotic name and settled on Häagen-Dazs. It doesn't mean anything.'

I knew far too much about the whole enterprise and said thanks to Liz. She added,
'Mind yourself, won't you?'
God preserve her, the dote.

21

*'I only know
The heart exists
On what
It daren't lose.'*

Fear, KB

I walked up St Patrick's Avenue with a certain amount of trepidation, passing the stalker's house, half expecting him to rush out. But all was quiet, if not on the Western Front, then in the avenue. At the church, I checked my watch – ten twenty-five – and noticed a guy sitting against the wall. Malachy wouldn't be pleased to see him there. The sun was shining but a cold drop was in the air. The guy, dressed in denim, with a red kerchief round his neck which said he was French or affected, was reading a book and glanced up at my approach, said,

'G'day mate.'

Australian.

I nodded and he held up the book, Eoin Colfer's *Artemis Fowl*, said,

'Hell of a book.'

I asked,

'Aren't you cold there?'

Not that I gave a toss. He stretched, said,

'Me? Don't feel the cold. Ireland doesn't really do cold, does it?'

Did my bit for the tourist board, said,

'Not with any intent.'

He put the book away, said,

'Got to get me some tucker. Recommend any place?'

'The Puckan, on Forster Street, they do huge fry-ups.'

He licked his lips, rubbed his palms together, said,

'Beauty, that'll do me. See you, mate.'

And he was gone, his kerchief blowing in the wind, which reminded me of the rumour that Bob Dylan was coming to Galway next summer. Him I'd pay serious cash to see. I liked him because he was older than me. As long as Bob stayed ahead in age, I wasn't yet due for the knacker's yard. Mass let out and a trickle began to emerge, mainly old people, not looking very uplifted. I guess Malachy wasn't the most charismatic of preachers. Ten minutes passed and I began to fret about the ice cream melting. Malachy appeared in a cloud of smoke and gruffness, breezed past me and, when I didn't follow, turned and barked,

'Are you coming or not?'

'Don't we do hellos, a pretence of civility?'

He threw his cigarette away and immediately lit another, said,

'I'm not feeling very civil.'

'Gee, that's new.'

I fell into step beside him and we headed for College Road. He glanced at the Roche's bag, said,

'That better not be alcohol.'

'It's ice cream, not that it's any of your business.'

He stared at me, said,

'It's ten thirty in the morning, who eats it at that hour?'

I wanted to bash his ears, said,

'I heard she likes a treat.'

He didn't answer. We stopped at a house halfway up the hill and he asked,

'Why don't you drop this whole thing?'

I told him the truth. As Sean Connery said, you do that, then it's their problem.

'I can't.'

He put a key in the door, said,

'Well, I'll be present during . . . the . . . interrogation. Bear in mind the poor woman is over seventy.'

I caught his wrist, didn't dilute the anger in my voice, said,

'You bear in mind a priest was beheaded and she knew the carry on of him. And no, you won't be present. Do I have to threaten you again with the newspapers?'

We entered a small lounge with a huge picture of the Sacred Heart on the wall. The wooden floor was spotless, shining even. He roared,

'Sister, we're here.'

Cautioned me,

'Mind your manners.'

I heard quiet footsteps and the nun came in. She was so nunnish, it was like a caricature. Wearing a heavy habit, with large silver crucifix adorning the front, the figure on the cross in ferocious agony. The habit was all the way to her shoes, those tiny black patent ones, not unlike the dancers in Riverdance. Her face was lineless, a beautiful complexion and blue troubled eyes. She was slightly stooped and gave a tiny smile, fear definitely in there. Malachy said,

'Good morning, Sister. This is Jack Taylor, he just wants a few minutes of your time.'

I was amazed at his voice, not pleading but gentle, as if he was speaking to a backward, shy child. She looked at us, then asked,

'Would ye like some tea? There's a pot made and some soda bread, fresh from the oven.'

To rile Malachy, I nearly asked for a large Jameson, but he said,

'I'll be in the next room. You call, Sister, when you're ready.'

Alarm hit her face as she realized she was going to be alone with me. He glared in my direction, patted her hand and left. I waited a moment then offered the soggy bag, said,

'I was told you have a taste for this.'

She took the bag, didn't look in it, said,

'You shouldn't have gone to any trouble, but God bless you, please take a seat.'

I did. She remained standing, poised for flight. I asked,

'You knew Father Joyce, knew him well?'

No point in fucking around, I was on the clock and Malachy could pull the plug any minute. She winced, agreed she did. She wouldn't meet my eyes and that irritated me, so I decided to focus her fast, rasped,

'You were aware of what he was doing to those boys, the altar lads?'

Do nuns lie? I don't see why not, but they probably

don't have a whole lot of opportunity. She gave a deep sigh, nodded. I had expected excuses. She was obviously using Sean Connery's dictum too. I added some steel to my tone, said,

'And you did nothing. You let him destroy those young people and you, what, watched?'

More harsh than I intended. Her face near crumpled and I saw tears in the corner of her eyes, but that wasn't going to cut it. I added,

'Who are the tears for, yourself or the piece of garbage who called himself a priest?'

Now she looked at me and with a hint of anger in those blue eyes said,

'It was different then, you have to understand . . .'

I snapped,

'Whoah, Sister, don't tell me what I have to do. It's a little late in the day for you to be decisive.'

She recoiled, my anger like something she had to physically move away from. The Lord knows, I've acted from rage far too often and the consequences have been ferocious. Spitting anger has informed most of my life, but the white-hot aggression I felt towards this old woman was new to me and I couldn't rein it in. I wanted to make a dent in her ecclesiastical armour, force her to acknowledge her complicity.

I deliberately lowered my voice lest Malachy came charging in. I wasn't finished with the poor creature yet, no way. I near spat,

'When the Guards were investigating the murder, didn't you feel compelled to contact them?'

She blessed herself, as if the ritual would protect her, muttered in Irish, *Mathair an Iosa* . . . Mother of Jesus. She answered,

'It wasn't my place.'

I let her see the disgust in my face, asked,

'And when the boys, the men, took action against the priest, when they made their claims of abuse, didn't you feel you could speak then, or was it still *not your place?*'

She was in agony. I couldn't care less, continued,

'One of the boys, the one who loved to feed the swans, didn't you think you could at least comfort him?'

Her eyes were weeping, her body giving silent shudders, and she said,

'The poor lad, he was so small. I offered him chocolate.'

I exploded.

'Chocolate! God Almighty, how magnificent of you! And that helped, did it? I'd say it really made everything OK. The next time the priest buggered him, he could think of chocolate, that it?'

The B-word near unravelled her and she got a look of total terror, as if she was re-living that moment, as if she could still see it. Maybe she could. She said,

'He had a reaction, as if he was going to faint. His whole body shook, his eyes sunk in his head . . .'

I cut her off, asked,

'But you were able to ignore that, just carry on, business as usual, get those floors polished, arrange the flowers on the altar, really *vital* shit?'

I could hear Malachy coming – time up. She said,

'I see that boy every day of my life.'

Then, as if she was gripped by prophecy, her eyes rolled in her head, like the visionaries do or the Ulster politicians in full flight, incanted,

'A beheading . . . look to the Bible . . . Salome, the woman . . . the woman it is you want.'

I turned away from her, muttered,

'Blast you to hell.'

She had her head bowed, indicated the now sodden Roche's bag, said,

'Thank you for that.'

As Malachy hit the threshold, I said low enough for her, just her,

'I hope it chokes you.'

Outside, Malachy asked,

'Well, did you get what you came for?'

I felt soiled, quipped,

'I think it went rather well.'

He lit a cigarette, stared at me, then,

'I've never held a high opinion of you, but I never had you as a cleric-hater.'

To which I had no answer, asked,

'You ever know a Father Gerald?' and described him.

He waved his hand in dismissal.

'Ah, a dipsomaniac, a rummy, a soak – like you, actually.'

When I didn't rise to the bait, he added,

'The man was brilliant, you know. Had a posting in the Vatican, could have gone all the way – the red hat, even.

But something happened. There was talk of an exorcism, but I don't put any stock in that. Like you, he was just feckless, pissed it all away. Alkies, you can't save them, they're the Devil's own.'

I was too tired to go the distance and asked,

'You ever listen to Steve Earle?'

22

'Look upon me if I lie.'

Pascal, *Pensées*, 811

'When the missionaries came to Africa, they had the Bible and we had the land. They said "Let us pray." We closed our eyes. When we opened them, we had the Bible and they had the land.'

This was said by Archbishop Tutu on a little historical irony in his country. I wish I'd remembered it when Malachy accused me of anti-clericalism.

There was a time, I'd been involved with the girls of the Magdalen Laundry. I'd been almost a regular Mass-goer, and if I remember, I wasn't drinking or smoking . . . Christ, what happened to me? The Mass had been a feature of regular comfort, a routine so alien I'd derived an almost peace. In Ireland, when an event of astonishing proportion occurs, we say, *There must be a rib broke in the Devil.*

His ribs seemed to be restored. The nun had mentioned the Bible – well, darkness was certainly stalking the land and a plague was upon our house.

Going after the nun, and going after her hard, made me feel cranked, but the downside comes and I had to ask,

'You beat up on an old nun, what the hell is that about?'

The answer is/was . . . rage.

Give me a few more minutes and I'd have been lashing out at her with fists. God Almighty, how far had I fallen? What next, mug old folk in their lonely homes? I needed a drink and badly. Heard my name called and here was Cody, carrying a large paper bag with the Brown Thomas logo on the front. What this said was 'money'.

He had that bashful look and near stammered,

'I hope I'm not out of line, but there was a sale in BTs and I had a few bob. I got this for you.'

He seemed mortified, pushed the bag at me and said,

'Don't be mad.'

And legged it.

It was a brown, three-quarter-length leather jacket, loads of pockets and on the front it said . . . *Boss*.

I came as close to weeping in the street as I've ever been. You do that in Ireland and they think,

'He started early.'

The hell with the shitty timetable, this was an emergency. I headed for Coyle's but got sidetracked – met Bobby, a man I'd helped out a long time ago. I couldn't recall what exactly I did but he seemed eternally grateful, grabbed my arm, said,

'You've got to come for a jar.'

We chanced O'Neachtain's, not a pub I'd frequent. Nothing wrong with it, in fact it has a lot going for it – old, has character – the problem is I know too many of the regulars, not a good idea for an alkie. Anonymity, even in your home town, has to be nourished, any small pocket you can carve, you do. Barely in the door and a near chorus of *Hiya Jack* began. Bobby ordered two pints of stout, Jameson chasers, and I decided to let the day go to ruin. We moved to a snug that shielded us from sight and we clinked glasses. *I, yet again, didn't touch the booze, just stared at it.* Bobby, already two sheets to the ferocious wind, didn't notice. He said,

'I had a win on the Lotto.'

He was my age, well shattered from poteen, betting offices and a wife with a motor mouth. A cast in his right eye gave you the impression he was constantly winking, and it was disconcerting at the best of times. A few drinks, you winked back.

I didn't know how much Bobby had won on the Lotto, but I guessed a bundle as various people made a point of sticking their heads over the partition and asking,

'How you doing, Bobby? Want a pint, want crisps, peanuts?'

And he had the scent of money, that intangible aura of a winner, and if you could get close to him, have him know you, it might rub off.

He gave me a radiant smile, white smudge on his lip from the Guinness. He knew I understood, said,

'Wankers, wouldn't give me the time of day before.'

I said,

'Couldn't happen to a nicer fella.'

I think I meant it, but good luck, you're never sure if you're not just the tiniest bit pissed that it ain't you. He drank deep, belched, asked,

'You OK for a few bob?'

Then laughed, said,

'A few bob from Bobby, that's rich – oops, another pun, two for one.'

I gave the polite laugh that suggests we move quickly on from this very unfunny line and said,

'No, I'm good, thanks for asking.'

His face got grave and I wondered if I'd insulted him. He leaned close, said,

'I don't want those bowsies to hear, there's a guy shouting the odds about doing you.'

I kept my alarm low and asked,

'Who, why . . . and especially where?'

I could smell his breath, the whiskey, the stout and . . . cheese? He said,

'Some Dublin git, he says he's going to get a high-powered rifle and take you down.'

It sounded so American I laughed and said,

'I know who it is, a pervert who was stalking a friend of mine. He's all mouth, nothing to worry about.'

Bobby didn't seem to agree, kept his concerned look, said,

'Jesus, Jack, a fella is talking about rifles, you have to pay heed.'

I was truly amused and said,

'Pub talk. I only worry about the guys who don't talk about it and do get a rifle. Now that's worth noting.'

Unbidden, the barman brought a fresh tray of drinks. When you win big, that's the type of thing that happens, they know you're good for it. Bobby changed tack, asked,

'Want to know how much I won?'

Did I?

'Only if you want to tell me.'

He did.

'Three-quarters of a mil . . .'

I whistled. He deserved it. Bobby was a guy who hadn't had two pennies to jiggle on a tombstone, a life of scrimping and scraping, keeping the wolf from the door, dodging the rentman, putting everything on the slate and living from pillar to post.

I was glad for him.

He asked,

'Guess how many millionaires the Lotto has made in Ireland?'

I had no idea, but he expected an answer, an attempt. He was paying the freight so I said,

'Am . . . a hundred?'

'Eight hundred and fifty. Oh, fifty and three-quarters, if you include me.'

What do you say? I said the obvious,

'Fuck.'

He was delighted, drank near half his fresh pint, said,

'The newspaper did a survey on winners, and guess how many of them were happy, happy they won it?'

Tough question.

'All of the lucky fuckers.'

He loved that, it was the right answer, in so far as it was the one he wanted. He exclaimed,

'Almost none. Said it ruined their lives. Know why?'

This I knew.

'Relatives.'

He was surprised, took a swig of Jameson to recoup, then,

'You're right. Caused ructions.'

So I had to ask,

'And with you, did it cause . . . ructions?'

His face fell and he looked on the verge of tears, said,

'My wife got a heart attack two weeks after, isn't that a whore of a thing?'

To put it mildly. I asked,

'How is she now?'

'Buried.'

Jesus.

He added,

'In a very expensive casket, not that it matters a toss.'

We were silent then, staring at our drinks, pondering the vagaries of life, the sheer unfairness. Then he brightened, said,

'I'm going to the Bahamas.'

'Good for you.'

'Want to come?'

Did I ever, said,

'God, I'd love to, but I'm caught up in something here. Great offer, though.'

He looked into his empty glass, then,

'I'll probably never go. I've never been anywhere, what would I do? . . . Drink . . . I can do that here and at least I know the pint is solid.'

Words to mark the wisdom of the ages.

My cue to leave. The conversation was dipping into serious maudlin territory and wouldn't improve so I stood, said,

'Thanks a million. Oh, three-quarters anyway.'

He liked that a lot, actually shook hands with me, said, 'I always liked you, Jack, even when you were a Guard.'

I looked at the untouched drink I was leaving behind. No doubt, I was seriously in need of treatment.

As I left, I saw a crowd of fellas saunter in, join him, telling him he was the best in the world.

As I headed across the Salmon Weir Bridge, I remembered the old name for it, the Bridge of Sighs, as it was the route from the courthouse to the old jail. I added my own small sigh to the generations that had gone before. Helped in no small measure by the tiny silver swan I could trace in the pocket of my jacket.

The next day I was hurting. You can't be Irish and curse a nun and not hurt. And there was the ever-present rage for Michael Clare and his – what do the Americans call it? – *dissing* of me.

Still hoping to find Jeff, I was perched on a bench in Eyre Square, my leather creaking in its newness, the winos stirring to my right, a cluster preparing to swoop on some likely soft touch.

Eyre Square: my whole history and the history of the city enclosed here. In 1963, I was hoisted by my father to catch a glimpse of John F. Kennedy as he and Jackie passed in a motor parade. The very same car that in Dallas he would ride in for the last time. The Irish loved him. He seemed to shine, maybe he did, and no matter how his name was tarnished now, he was among our hierarchy. I'd once heard an old Claddagh woman say,

'His halo still shines.'

Only Bill Clinton would grab the same slice of the Irish heart.

In the Middle Ages, this was a green just outside the main wall. The square was named for the mayor who in 1710 gave the land to the city. Now it contains Kennedy Park.

I stared at the rust-coloured fountain, built to celebrate the five-hundredth anniversary of the incorporation of the city. It has sails to represent the Hooker ships that built the trade of the city. Always amuses Americans, who go,

'Hookers!'

Add that we call cigarettes *fags*, and they are, dare I say, *hooked*. Behind me was Brown's Doorway, from the seventeenth century, a reminder of the fourteen tribes that once ruled the town.

Maybe my favourite feature are the cannons from the Crimean War. They stand like UN observers, useless and obvious, serving nothing. The statue of our poet Padraig O'Conaire, a man fond of a bevy too, was about to be moved. The whole area was going to be revamped, Padraig consigned to a building site for eighteen months, alone and neglected, like the decent poets. He wrote in Irish, guaranteeing that he'd never be read. A woman with a young girl strolled by. The woman looked at me and I smiled. The little girl shouted at me,

'Smile at your own wife.'

Even at that young age, Irish females are feisty, ready to bust your chops before you utter a word. They need to learn early to deal with the sulkiness of the male. I rubbed the patch on my arm, marvelling that with all the freight I'd been carrying, I hadn't yet smoked. I'm loath to term it a miracle, but it was astonishing. A man was approaching, wearing a very battered leather coat. For one mad moment, I thought it might be the coat I'd brought back from London which had been stolen long ago. Shook my head, as if it was a mirage. The man recognized me and stopped.

Trade. The owner/barman from Coyle's.

It was like seeing a vampire at noon. His face had the mottle of the habitual drinker. He was wearing a black tie, white shirt, black pants, looked almost respectable till you met the eyes and saw the faded life.

I asked,

'How you doing?'

Sounding like Joey from *Friends*, which is not really to be recommended, if you're Irish. He appraised me. If he saw something he liked, he wasn't showing it. He asked,

'Join you for a minute?'

I moved over on the bench and he sat down. He smelled of hops and barley, which figures if you're in the bar game. He put his hand in his pocket, produced a pipe, a leather pouch of tobacco and fired up, took his own time in getting it lit, gave a sigh of contentment. The aroma was sweet but not cloying and he said,

'Clan.'

The brand.

He stared at the jacket, said,

'Cost a few punts, that.'

'Euros.'

He was not a man who liked being corrected and I made a note of it. He answered,

'Euros, punts, none of it worth a toss.'

I said,
'My son gave it to me.'
Took him by surprise and he thought about it, then,
'I don't have a family, never wanted to give up me freedom. What's he do, your lad?'
My lad.
Without missing a beat I said,
'He's in computers.'
He muttered there was a future in that, but not with any conviction.
We sat in silence, surveying the square, then he said,
'I'm coming from a funeral.'
Explained the attire. I did the Irish thing, asked,
'Anyone close?'
He was not a man who answered quickly. As if he searched for hidden agendas, then,
'Who's close?'
I wished I had a cig, asked,
'Was he a friend?'
I was thinking, why the hell don't I shut up? He didn't answer for a full five minutes. I know, I counted every awkward one. Then,
'A customer.'
I was surprised and gave a grunt of assent. He turned to me, said,
'You knew him.'
'Did I?'
'The priest, Gerald.'
And I remembered Gerald saying,
'The Devil's right hand.'

Gave me a spooky feeling, though it could have been the need for a drink. I said,

'I'm sorry.'

He nodded as if he expected nothing less, then,

'The bastards wouldn't bury him, so I shelled out.'

I presumed he meant the Church and said,

'That was good of you.'

He stood, shook the ashes out of his pipe, banged it against the bench, said,

'Don't talk shite.'

We let that gem swirl above our heads. Then he gave me a full look, said,

'You're a quare one.'

Not in the sense of gay, but more the Behan meaning of *odd*. Before I could, as it were, rise to the occasion, he asked,

'What kind of man goes to the pub, pays good money for whiskey and then doesn't touch a drop?'

Did I want to explain to him it was my deal with God? No.

When he saw no answer was coming, he shrugged, said,

'No skin off my nose.'

And walked away.

I wanted to roar,

'Thanks for sharing.'

But I was afraid he'd come back. I sat for another twenty minutes. I'd liked that priest a lot. One meeting and I felt like I knew him. Tried to find some prayer. A wino approached and I gave him ten euro, felt that was the best prayer of all.

* * *

Next morning, I was up early, got the phone directory and rang Michael Clare. A woman answered.

'Michael Clare's, Engineers, how may I help?'

'I'd like to speak to Michael, please.'

Step on those manners.

'May I say who's calling?'

'Father Joyce.'

If she recognized the murdered man's name, she kept it to herself, said,

'One moment, please.'

Then like afterglow, added,

'Father.'

He came on, caution in his voice, said,

'Hello?'

'Mike, it's Jack Taylor.'

A moment, then,

'Ah, the private dick . . . The Father Joyce bit, that supposed to be what? Ironic?'

'I don't do irony.'

He let out a suppressed breath.

'What is it, Taylor?'

'What happened to Jack?'

'Listen, Taylor, I'm a busy man and you're clearly an idiot. Either get to it or—'

'I want to buy you lunch.'

'What?'

'So, are you up for a spot of lunch?'

Exasperation in his tone, he asked,

'Why on earth would I have lunch with you?'

Time to get ol' Michael focused, said,

'Met your sister.'

Huge intake of breath, then the palpable rage.

'You stay the fuck away from my sister.'

I ignored that, continued,

'Here's some hard ball. If you don't meet me, I'll make some phone calls, tell that flash receptionist her boss cut a priest's head off, and you know what, I had me a talk with a nun and she got me thinking, maybe your sister beheaded the priest?'

He went quiet, then agreed to a drink that evening in Brennan's Yard, six thirty, and he slammed the phone down. It rang almost immediately. Vinny from Charly Byrnes' bookshop.

'Jack, me oul' segotia, it's Vinny.'

'How are you doing, Vinny?'

'Good. Reason I'm calling is, we got a load of new books – a lot of crime – and among them David Goodis, Dan Simmons and other gems.'

I was amazed.

'I thought it was impossible to get Goodis?'

'It is, but you know us, we like a challenge.'

'That's great, I'll be in.'

'Don't sweat it, I'll put them aside for you.'

A dark coincidence, in that time of shadows, that those books should come along. I was too far out on the edge to read, or to read anything significant into this happening. My existence had become so haphazard, the odd had become the norm.

* * *

In 1953, at the age of thirty-three, following a prolific New York career as a pulp writer, David Goodis returned home to live with his parents in Philadelphia. He became a virtual recluse.

His lifestyle was beyond strange. In California, he rented a sofa in a friend's house for four dollars a month and would crash there intermittently, when he was on the prowl. Prowling for the fat black hookers he paid to humiliate him. Wore suits till they were threadbare, then dyed them blue and went right on wearing them. Recycling before his time.

A habit he had, taking the red cellophane from cigarette packets, shoving it up his nose, pretending to have nose-bleeds. How fucking weird is that? Then he'd howl from pain. Thing is, he'd have slotted right into Coyle's.

This was a writer with a six-year contract from Warner Brothers, published his first novel at twenty-one, and at twenty-eight years of age his most famous book, *Dark Passage*, was sold as a Bogart/Bacall vehicle.

After the death of his father, Goodis began to lose it, big time. When his mother died, he was truly gone, lost. He sued the producers of *The Fugitive*, believing they had stolen his work. He ended up in the asylum, and at the age of forty-nine he was dead.

23

'Christianity is strange;
it bids man to recognize he is vile
and even abominable.'

Pascal, *Pensées*, 537

Every day, I tried to listen to the news, to keep some anchor on reality, reasoning if I knew what was going on then I wasn't entirely gone.

Ireland prided itself on being

> Confident
>
> Aware
>
> Modern.

Our image abroad was that of hip coolness. We were, in the words of the culture, a *happening* place. Imagining we'd moved far from the provincial, closed, parochial society of the bad years, events were occurring to remind us we hadn't moved as far or as fast as we thought.

A story that beggared belief that day.

Health workers, checking on a house, found a woman dead in her bed. Not only had she been dead a year, but her sister slept in the same bed! Said she never realized, thought her sister was just ill. A brother, living in the same tiny abode, said,

'I thought she was pretending.'

A photo of the poor bastard in all the papers showed a

face of ancient bewilderment, not unlike the faces of the hordes who sailed to America in the coffin ships during the famine.

My beard was coming in, if not my ship. Coming in grey and wretched. Told myself I looked like an artist and muttered,

'Piss artist.'

For the meeting with Michael Clare, I wore the new jacket from Cody, a white shirt and a tie, loosely knotted to convey nonchalance, and cleanish white cords. All I needed was a yacht and I'd be the total asshole, glass of Pimm's in my hand to complete the portrait. The pants were slightly short so I wore boots, hoped to offset the discrepancy.

Didn't.

Splashed on the Polo aftershave and was, if not present-able, at least aromatic. Asked myself why I was meeting him a second time. He'd already confessed, albeit solely to me. What I wanted was for him to confess publicly. That way, I'd be spitting in the eyes of the unholy trinity, sticking it to Clancy, the Church, Malachy. My weapon was Kate. If he thought I'd float the story about his sister being a suspect, he might come forward to save her. The bouncer guy had said he'd do anything for her. I didn't think for a moment the nun would go public on a woman being capable of the decapitation. I only needed Clare to think she might.

On my way, I met a Romanian named Caz. We had a fractured relationship. The odd times we met, I'd give him a few euro, till, as he said, he *got his shit together*. He was fond of this phrase and used it as often as he could. I ran into him outside the Quays, music coming loud from there.

Sounded like a punk version of 'Galway Bay', which is a step beyond articulation. He greeted me with energy.

'Jack, great to see you.'

Hard to say if he was entering or exiting the pub. He'd been in Galway five years and mastered a form of Irish-English that wasn't always easy to follow. I said,

'Caz.'

For a horrible moment, I thought he was going to hug me, which would suggest he was exiting the pub or simply being European. So I quickly palmed him a few notes. He said, as he put them away,

'Ah Jack, you're mighty, you know I'm good for it.'

Yeah.

Then he leaned close, said,

'I hear you're on the piss.'

He wouldn't have mentioned that before I parted with the cash, but he'd nothing to lose or gain now. I asked,

'Has anybody seen me put a glass to my lips?'

That was way too intense, too intellectual a question, so he ignored it. As I mentioned, he'd been in Ireland for five years so knew how to play the verbal combat. He looked back at the Quays, asked,

'You want one now, my shout?'

Which it would be. He'd shout for the drinks then go to the toilet as payment loomed. I said,

'I'd love to but I've got to meet someone.'

He didn't believe a word, looked down the street towards Spanish Arch, said,

'They say you're drinking in Coyle's.'

I didn't deny or confirm. He touched my shoulder, went,

'You be careful, my friend, it's a bad place.'
He was quiet, then,
'What's this about you having a son?'
I shrugged, said,
'People blowing smoke.'
He digested that, then asked if I knew they'd deported
eighty-eight non-nationals and more were to follow.
I said I hadn't heard, asked,
'And you, are you on the list?'
He shrugged, said,
'We're all on a list.'
This was a little too deep for me so I probed,
'Are you legal?'
He got angry, almost petulant, replied,
'I'm getting my shit together.'

I like Brennan's Yard. It has an air of class without notions
and you can always get a seat. It used to be literally a yard.
For bizarre reasons, when they built the hotel, they kept
the name. At first it confused people, but had now been
assimilated into the life of the city.

Michael Clare was at a table near the door, dressed in
another impressive suit, and was if possible even better
looking. I rubbed my scraggy beard and felt shabby. He
had his legs stretched out, seemed to be totally at ease. I
approached, asked,
'Waiting long?'
He indicated his glass, it had some sort of pink liquid,
said,
'Haven't touched my Campari and soda.'

I guess a pint of Guinness would have clashed with his suit. I got a diet coke and joined him. The surroundings were some contrast to Coyle's, but I didn't share that. He examined me, my beard, tired eyes, said,

'Been having some late nights, huh?'

What do you do, plead guilty? I said nothing and he asked,

'How is the new apartment?'

Got me.

Before I could form a reply, a family came in, took the table directly in our line of vision. Young parents with two boys aged around ten. He took a sip of his mouthwash, his eyes riveted on the family. I was at a loss. Where to begin?

My plan had seemed fine in my head. All I had to do was threaten him with my continued harassment of him and his sister and hey presto, he'd agree to come forth, tell the world he was the priest killer. Now it seemed to be the height of folly.

Sitting with this confident, urbane man, my resolve faltered. One of the boys produced a bar of chocolate, began to shove chunks into his mouth. Clare fixed on him, seemed mesmerized by the action. A sheen of perspiration popped out on his brow and the blood, literally, left his face. I asked,

'You OK?'

He emitted a small whimper, a sound I'll never forget. Then his eyes rolled back in his head. It was so sudden, dramatic, that I sat immobile till I realized he'd passed out. I leaned over, loosened his tie, began to tap his face. He groaned, and in the voice of a young child muttered,

'My bum hurts.'

I said,

'Stay there.'

Went and got a brandy, brought it back, held his head, got the glass to his blue lips, slurped it in. The family were staring open-mouthed. The woman whispered to the husband and they stood, got the hell out. The brandy began to restore colour to his face and he sat upright. I said,

'Maybe put your head between your knees.'

He waved that away, said,

'I'm coming out of it. In a minute I'll be OK. You can't drag my sister into this, I'll do anything to keep her sheltered.'

He was coming out of it.

He took another taste of the brandy, nodded.

I was seriously confused. If he could have such a reaction in public, what must he suffer in private? My conscience pleaded,

'He's suffered enough – is suffering. Leave him the fuck be.'

Whatever justice I'd envisaged being dealt out to him, how could it offset the price he'd already paid? His composure was near full restored. He asked,

'So, Jack, what is it you wanted to see me about?'

I shook my head, said,

'It doesn't matter now.'

He raised an eyebrow, said,

'You're a strange man, Jack. I thought you were going to pressurize me, to attempt to get me to . . . how shall I phrase it . . . go public? There isn't anything I wouldn't do for her. I'd give my own life to safeguard her.'

My glass was empty, echoing my heart. I was toying with heading to the counter for another. He smiled and I asked,

'How did you know where I live?'

He gave a brief smile, no warmth, said,

'You check up on me, visit my sister for Chrissakes, you don't think I'd do the same?'

The nun's words were ringing in my head. The old people used to say *the devil was in me*, and the only exorcist I knew was dead, so I blurted,

'Would your sister kill for you?'

He gave a long sigh, shook his head, then said,

'I think so, but she didn't kill the priest. She is strong enough, but you know that, you've seen her hands. She might go after the nun. I always kind of thought she would, but only if she could use her beloved rifle . . . Now me, if I harboured any such thoughts towards the merciless nun, I'd drown the bitch.'

The words were chilling in their low tone.

I got a longing for Coyle's. Brennan's Yard was not my place. He asked,

'You wired, Jack? Got a tape on me?'

My turn to smile, if of the bitter variety, said,

'Only in the movies. But I'm wired all right, though not in the sense you mean.'

I was about to get up, order another coke, when he said,

'The nun?'

I pretended not to hear, stalling for time, went,

'What?'

'The priest, Joyce, he was the boss, but she . . . she ran everything, took care of the sacristy, knew how things worked. Shit, made them work.'

Took me a moment to see where this was going, then I asked,

'She knew what was going on?'

He nodded, a picture of resigned acceptance, said,

'Sister Mary Joseph – she loved ice cream. I went to her for help, can you believe it?'

He wasn't expecting an answer and I didn't attempt one. He continued,

'Like she was going to betray her idol. She boxed my ears. Ice cream, she got off on it. I guess if you forsake all other pleasures, what remains contains the heat of all the others.'

Who was I to argue? He asked,

'Do you remember your description of *brave* . . . the time you were in my office, you were describing the bronze bull?'

I nodded, seeing John Behan's beautiful craft. He asked,

'You think there's any bravery any more?'

I didn't, but for something to say, said,

'Yeah, maybe. When you do the one thing you don't want to do, that you should have done a long time ago.'

He was considering something. Then,

'I had this vision, this grand city on the Corrib, the city of the tribes that would be the equal of anywhere on earth. My father would have been proud, but you know what, Jack?'

I didn't, so didn't say anything. He continued,

'Every great vision requires a great sacrifice, and to see your vision fulfilled, to burn so that it can be realized, that might be worth a man's life. Do you think that is possible? And if you save your sister too – that's worth a life, you think? If that nun makes those allegations, my sister would be destroyed. My father never liked me, but on his deathbed he made me promise, no matter what the cost, I was to mind her.'

I wish now I'd said anything else, but oh God, here is what I said.

'Your father is dead.'

He may have added,

'Not to me.'

But that's probably fanciful. I only know his speech would burn my soul.

I stood, time to head, and he stared at me, then,

'You think, Jack, given a different set of circumstances, we might have been friends?'

I told the truth, fuck it.

'No.'

He held out his hand, more in hope than anticipation, said,

'Good luck, Jack.'

Then,

'I like the jacket. Hugo Boss, is it?'

I took his hand, felt the wetness from anxiety, said,

'Good luck to you, too.'

His face spread in a wide grin.

'I think it's a little late for me, but thanks for the sentiment.'

24

'*Piety is different from superstition.*'

Pascal, *Pensées*, 255

The man had lured the nun with the promise of money for the Church. He strangled her in the car – it didn't take long, she seemed to almost accept it with resignation, no struggle, as if it was the penance she'd been waiting for.

He muttered,

'You had to mention my sister, didn't you? You crowd, you think you can destroy anyone you like.'

In the early hours of the morning, he'd taken her body to Spanish Arch. It was quiet then, nobody around, all the action across the water in Quay Street. Only the swans paid attention, as if he'd come to feed them. In a way he had.

He let her slide into the water and four swans swam over to investigate. He watched for a moment as she slipped beneath the water, a swan dipping its beak with short furious movements at the nun's habit.

Then he turned quickly, got in his car, headed out of the city.

There was a granite wall past Spiddal, built in penal times and still as solid as hatred. He accelerated as he approached, not seeing the wall but a grand city, his city, perhaps a bronze statue by John Behan commemorating the man who'd brought it about, *a veritable emperor, who'd given his life for it*, the shining light in the darkness of Europe. He screamed,

'The Emperor of Ice Cream.'

The car hit the wall at over a hundred miles an hour, the impact waking people from miles around.

I riffled through the books Vinny had given me. It was a long time before I'd examined the full range of titles Vinny had provided, and nigh lost among the mysteries was this: Blake Morrison's *And When Did You Last See Your Father?*

I selected some poetry and tried to read, but what poet, what lines? I can't recall. I do remember believing I'd found the answer to anxiety. Gave the credit to literature and didn't acknowledge the dual longing in my heart for a child and yes, whisper it . . . Ridge. Still having dreams of her. I thought those dreams were the reason I was feeling feverish, worn out, wheezy. Got some Night Nurse, the pharmacist cautioning,

'Don't mix alcohol with that.'

Oh gee, really?

Doesn't get any more Irish than that.

I caught a bad bout of flu. I'm not saying it was connected to reading poetry, but books are dangerous, ask any redneck.

I'd no idea where my investigation had been going to take me, save the docks. I went into a sort of emotional meltdown, as if I was behind glass. Nothing really registering, like I was a spectator at events that were unfolding and I was powerless to prevent.

Maybe it was a blessing in disguise. Once I heard a woman in Claddagh roar,

'Can I just have one lousy blessing that's not in disguise?'

What saved me from total fade was Cody. He arrived at my apartment, waving tickets.

'I've got us the stand for the match.'

The match.

The much-heralded hurling game. I didn't want to go, but Cody said,

'I'm ashamed to admit it, but I don't know much about hurling. Will you explain it?'

So I went, and had a great day.

Great days and me are not often in the same sentence, much less the same neighbourhood. The day was one of those gorgeous crisp fresh ones, the type of day when you think that everything is going to be OK, not wonderful but in the zone. The match was a cracker. We roared like mad fellas, bought scarves and wore them with pride, had a fry-up in the Galleon, one of the last real cafés in the country.

When I was heading home, Cody saying he'd had a brilliant day, that it was *gifted, mighty*, I very nearly gave him a hug. I realized the fog had lifted. The psychic shutters that had been blinding me were up and light was streaming in.

What I remember about that day is seeing fathers with their sons at the game and feeling part of that. It was, I hate to say it, downright intoxicating.

Back at my apartment, I met removal men and then the

tenant who busted my balls. He tried to duck me. I asked,

'What's happening, bro?'

The *bro* was purely the bad drop in me. He tried to stand with his shoulders erect, but his face betrayed him, a blend of fear and trepidation. He said,

'I'm moving.'

So I went for it.

'Why?'

He nearly rose to indignation but flunked it, said,

'This neighbourhood is no longer what it was.'

I offered to take the box he was carrying but he held it like a rosary at a wake. Near hysterical, he shouted,

'I don't think your help is what I need.'

I smiled, kept moving, added,

'Drop a card when you land.'

He stared at me and I said,

'Gonna miss you, bro. Party animals are hard to find.'

Gave myself a new assignment: find Jeff, and maybe see if I could work up the courage to approach Cathy. It would occupy my mind. Then I rang Ridge and persuaded her to meet me for a coffee.

We met in Java's, neutral territory. I was amazed at how well she looked, dressed in a navy tracksuit, her eyes and hair shining. I said,

'*Dia go glor* (God be praised) . . . you look great.'

She smiled, said,

'I met someone.'

She was delighted I was using Irish, her language of birth. She inspected me – when an Irish woman does that, you are thoroughly scanned – went,

'You're sober.'

'Today, anyway.'

I was going to add the rider, *One more attempt, one more failure*, but it had a whine to it. We actually had a civilized chat, then she confessed,

'I never thought I'd hook up with anyone again.'

I was glad, genuinely so. Her hard edges were almost smooth. She leaned forward, said,

'I did some checking on the . . . stalker . . . He was once picked up for possession of a high-powered rifle, but the case got thrown out.'

I shrugged, said,

'He's gone. He got a serious wake-up call. The likes of him, they find a rock to hide under.'

She wasn't entirely convinced, said in Irish,

'*Bhi curamach* (be careful).'

Outside, we stood, surprised by the near intimacy we'd achieved. A cold wind was building. She commented,

'Winter's coming.'

I said,

'No biggie.'

And she laughed. Then we almost hugged. I said,

'Be seeing you, Ni Iomaire.'

She nodded, said,

'That'd be good.'

I kept going, picking up the pace, leaving her behind. The eerie bit, in my head was a priest I once heard in Christchurch singing the Exsultet . . . and a woman behind me going,

'Jaysus, that's only lovely.'

* * *

The next few days, I stayed home, unplugged the phone, didn't watch the news or listen to the radio. I just wanted time to rest, try and get some energy back. Got deep into reading. David Goodis, of course. Among the batch I got from Vinny was Eugene Izzi, his *Invasions* crammed between *Dark Passage* and *Cassidy's Girl*.

If ever a noir writer died a noir death, it was him. In Chicago, he was found dangling from the window of a fourteen-storey office block, wearing a bullet-proof vest. In his pockets were

>Brass knuckles
>
>Tear gas
>
>Threatening letters from a militia group.

The doors to his apartment were locked and a loaded gun lay beside his desk. Almost like a cosy English novel, but there the resemblance ended.

I could identify with the paranoia.

In my hand was the tiny silver swan.

A Tuesday morning, the feast of St Anthony, a knock at my door. I considered ignoring it, but if it was Ridge . . . well hell, I got up, opened the door. A guy, seriously winded, holding a parcel, wheezed,

'Man, this sucker is heavy . . . And them stairs?'

He paused, asked,

'You Jack Taylor?'

'Yes.'

'Thank Christ. I'd hate to have to lug this another yard.'

He handed the parcel to me and he was right, it had weight. I put it down and he produced a form, asked,

'Sign here.'

I did.

He mopped his brow and I offered him a drink, looking for my wallet to tip. He shrugged it off, said,

'Naw, I'd be pissing for a week.'

Which was a little more than I needed to know. He wouldn't take the tip either, said,

'Give it to the Poor Clares.'

I was going to tell him they'd a website but he was already wheezing away. I closed the door, put the parcel on the table, got a knife, tore the packing away, stood back.

John Behan's bronze bull.

Took me a moment before I saw the white card under the bull's feet. Picked it up. The lettering was in gothic script, read,

NUN
BUT
THE BRAVE.

25

'Men are so inevitably mad
that not to be mad would be to give
a mad twist to madness.'

Pascal, *Pensées*, 414

Malachy had come to my apartment, and to say I was stunned is putting it mildly. He said,

'I heard you had a new place so I brought a St Bridget's Cross to keep the home safe.'

I offered him tea and he snapped,

'Tea, you call that hospitality? Didn't you ever hear of whetting a man's whistle?'

I glared at him, said,

'There is no booze here.'

He lit up a cig, didn't ask if it was OK, despite me still on the patches. Then his eyes locked on the tiny silver swan nestling on the bookcase. He went,

'How on earth did you get that?'

I was confused, asked,

'What . . . why?'

He'd gone pale, no mean feat when you have red ruddy cheeks, said,

'In Father Joyce's hand, when they found his body, that . . . yoke . . . was clutched there.'

The room spun as the implications dawned. There had

only been two, both owned by Kate. I had to sit down, take a deep breath, then asked,

'The nun, Sister Mary Joseph, is she all right?'

He was angry, said,

'Ya eejit, she was found drowned. Must have fallen in when she was feeding the swans.'

I went for broke, asked,

'Michael Clare?'

'Him . . .'

His tone full of bile, he said,

'Crashed his car into a brick wall. Good riddance.'

And in an instant, it was clear. Michael Clare did for the nun, but Kate . . . Kate did for Father Joyce. She had the strength, and leaving the swan behind – a form of poetic justice? Her version of admission – not to the world, but to Michael. Or maybe she had been careless. You sever a person's head off, clear thinking is not going to be your strong suit.

I said,

'I'd like you to go now.'

'What? I just got here. Don't you want me to bless the rooms?'

I stood up, said,

'Shove your blessing.'

He considered squaring up, but said,

'You just don't have it in you to be civil, do you?'

Evelyn Waugh once said,

'You don't know how much nastier I would be if I hadn't become a Catholic.'

What I went with was Orwell's line,

'One cannot really be a Catholic and grown up.'

* * *

Nobody gets shot in Galway, I mean it just doesn't happen. Least not yet. We are supposedly getting Starbucks soon, so anything is possible, but gunplay, no. Give it a year and who knows?

We're not too far from the border and of course, theoretically, you could imagine on a clear fine night you can hear the sound.

But that's fanciful, and whatever else, we don't do a lot of wishful thinking. Knowing Kate went hunting pheasant, that the stalker had been arrested once for possession of a high-powered rifle, or that Cathy was mouthing off in the pubs about killing me didn't make me pause or check rooftops. I was so glad to be sober, to be out and not even smoking, guns were not on my agenda.

I wasn't unfamiliar with them but I was certainly not in the region where guns are expected.

Ridge had recently blessed me with,

'*Bhi curamach.*'

Means 'be careful' . . . I wish I'd listened to her.

I was out for an early-morning walk, early being ten thirty, working the limp out of my leg. Had strolled through the town and got a notion to see the ocean. Checked my watch and knew a bus was due to leave in the next ten minutes. I reached the top of Eyre Square when from nowhere Cody appeared, fell into step beside me on my left side, said, glancing at the leather jacket,

'You're the boss.'

I smiled and he added,

'I have a great idea for us.'

I never got to hear it.

I was thinking of my father, a time when my mother had been up to her usual shenanigans, causing havoc over the rent or some related issue. My father had whispered to me,

'She means well.'

Never ceases to amaze me how we excuse the most despicable behaviour with that lie, and I have never believed for one friggin' second that the mean-spirited *mean well*. But they do rely heavily on us excusing them and thus they have a mandate to continue their cycle of disguised malevolence. Cody, assuming I wasn't paying attention, moved to my right side, blocking the sun.

I heard a crack, like the proverbial car backfiring.

Someone screamed,

'Jesus, there's a sniper . . .'

The very spot I'd been in, where Cody now stood, that's where the bullet hit. Took him in the chest. A second shot, tearing a hole an inch further up, and I remembered Cathy, her words,

'Can't seem to get that head shot, my aim is low.'

How fitting, I thought, that I was in Kennedy Park. A man was shouting,

'Call an ambulance!'

Blood splatters were strewn on my shiny jacket.

Then another voice, concerned, knowing, going,

'No, call . . . a . . . priest.'

There's irony for you. If I could have laughed, I would, but my throat was choked. I'd wanted to say,

'Well, this day is shot to hell.'

I knelt by Cody, his blood oozing through my hands. A woman behind me was keening, *Oh, Sweet Jesus*. She began to massage my shoulder – it annoyed me, a lot. There was slight pressure from Cody's hand, he was trying to squeeze mine but it was fading.

My eyes were wet. I thought first it was blood then realized it was tears. The woman was massaging my shoulder still and I heard her say to someone, I think I heard her say, *It's his son*. I do know she continued to knead my shoulder.